SPIRITUAL INCITEMENT

Audhu bi-llahi mina shaitani rajim
Bismillahir Rahmanir Rahim
La haula wala quwatta illa bi-llahi-l
`Aliyu-l `Azim

Serge and Roman Lapytski

authorHOUSE®

AuthorHouse™
1663 Liberty Drive
Bloomington, IN 47403
www.authorhouse.com
Phone: 1-800-839-8640

Published by AuthorHouse 12/26/2012

ISBN: 978-1-4817-0175-4 (sc)
ISBN: 978-1-4817-0174-7 (e)

Library of Congress Control Number: 2012924137

Acknowledgments from Serge

I would like to express a special Thank You to my charming, beautiful and joyful daughter Christina, who is always sharp, passionate, devoted and ready to help. Thank You Christina for your assistance in writing this book. And Thank You for everything else. You are the best.

Also, I would like to say Thank You to the entire AuthorHouse.com staff. You guys are amazing and real professionals.

My thanks and appreciation to:

You, The Reader, whom I always kept in mind while writing this book.

My wonderful sister Galina and my charming niece Marina, for their support and encouragement, Thank You very much! You are awesome!

My very lively auntie Zina and my cousin Evgeni. Thank You folks for the inspiration.

My friends, you gentlemen are fun and amazing.

TABLE OF CONTENTS

INTRODUCTION

"Spiritual Incitement…" is a psychological thriller with an intense focus on the unstable emotional state of a young gentleman named Romeo, who used to be very healthy and brave, before strange things started happening to him.

A couple of professionals, a Psychologist and an Intelligence Officer, by the will of fate or the solitary decision of their Boss, got involved in the complex investigation of the bizarre incidents while trying to help Romeo, the youthful chap who is the main character in the book, to get back on his feet and live a wonderful life. The story incorporates elements of mystery and drama, psychosomatic horror and the typical traits of the crime novel genre.

The sequence of events shows the struggle of Romeo to resolve conflicts with his own mind, which, in reality, is an effort to understand something that has happened to him. The investigators, while exploring both the known and unknown facts of that young man's life, are trying to stay open minded and reasonable, but still believe that all the events that took place are just a result of a very well planned and executed scheme.

Also, the book covers a number of interesting operations carried out by one Intelligence Service to outplay their opposition. Furthermore, there are some "wild" ideas for the use of a human Soul: when this "Spirit agent" crosses over into a different world, they see no borders, no boundaries, no walls... Their Soul can travel anywhere, and then communicate their findings back into this world. This will be a breakthrough for any party, who is able to discover or develop this "technology"...

ABOUT THE AUTHORS

Serge Lapytski is a graduate of Boston University, a former Military Officer and the author of "Cockroaches!", "Believe, Achieve and Forgive!", "Me and my life: guilty without guilt or confessions of the innocent" and "The heart of a lion! E-Hare". The books were published during 2009-12. Serge successfully completed many special programs at various educational institutions in Canada, England, Russia, the USA and some others. So far in total Serge visited twenty countries for didactic, business and pleasure purposes. To get more information about Serge's work please visit the www.lapytski.com website or www.google.com search engine and type Serge Lapytski in the search criteria field.

My son, Roman Lapytski, is a very young gentleman, in his early twenties, who already has his own views and opinions about life and world events. Roman came up with the idea of "Spiritual Incitement..." and inspired me to write this book. Moreover, Roman wrote some parts of it himself. Very energetic, humorous and having a positive attitude, this youthful man brings a lot of love and joy to his family and friends. We always love you Roman and Thank You for everything.

THE GOBLIN

"Serge, Boss wants to see you…"

It was Kristina, a new addition to the team of Intelligence agents, who entered into the office, or should I say, our working area. She had some flowers in her hands, probably another gift from her boyfriend. Almost every day he sends her flowers or chocolates or something else. Thanks dude, because of individuals like you, women become spoiled and us, men, have to suffer, be creative and find new ways and resources to make them happy. On the other hand, I was thankful to the guy for reminding me that I should better myself as a representative of the simple half of humanity.

Kristina is always in a good mood, elegant, young, attractive, and a very smart agent, she joined the Intelligence Service recently, after successfully graduating from some well known university with a degree in Psychology and she is professionally skilled in hypnosis as well.

Our office was quite big in size and we were sharing it with some other agents, totaling sixteen of us. The day started as usual for me: morning exercise, shower, breakfast, trip to the agency. I don't know about other people, but usually in the morning I have a pretty good picture in my mind of what to expect during the day. I get this information from my dreams. I guess if you pay attention to what you see at night and keep track of it every day, checking the meaning of your dreams in clever books, then, most likely, you will know what to expect and be ready for it both mentally and physically. And last night was no exception: I saw a dream where I started reading a new book. But the pages in the book were indistinct and I had to make an effort to read them.

When your Boss wants to see you, you better go right away, especially if you work for an organization like ours. Sometimes you can save the World, literary speaking, if you make it on time. I thanked Kristina for passing the message on to me and thinking "what is it regarding?" locked the file I was working on into the cabinet (it is a policy at our agency not to leave any job related materials unattended, not because we do not trust one another, on the opposite, but because we are professionals, we do not take that type of chance) and quickly moved to the Chief's office. It was not far away, just down the corridor.

Our Boss, director Goldberg, a fifty year old gentleman, good looking and well maintained, a real professional, took good care of himself and it was obvious to every one of us that he enjoyed expensive things. Every day he wore a new suit, sometimes I even wondered: "how many suits does he have?" A clean shirt, a tie and shoes always matched his overall attire. Add to it a classy Rolex watch, a pleasant looking and clean shaved face and you will get George Clooney himself.

Director Goldberg did not like "surprises" and he demanded from all the personnel to eliminate "that type of accident" in our every day job through analysis, anticipation of the upcoming events and preparation. This saved him and our workforce a lot of trouble. Also, he was good at reading people, just by looking at someone he could easily say what they were thinking about – a dangerous man overall.

After I knocked on his door and asked permission to enter he had that puzzled expression on his face that right away I said:

"Did you want to see me Sir?"

"Yes, and close the door", answered the director.

Usually, when I am called to the director's office, just to show him that I am confident and ready for whatever action required I would say:

"What did I do again?"

And the director would reply:

"It is not what you do or did; it is what you did not do..."

He was nice to me, and he always took advantage of my work attitude and my skills or aptitude by giving me more loads to carry than to the other agents. I did not mind that at all. But of course I would pretend that I am not happy with the new assignment and would bring it up to him that I already have five or six projects I am working on and that I am behind schedule already. Then the director would say:

"Who else, Serge? You are the best we have and we need results... And we need them fast. I will find the way to compensate you..."

Actually, to be totally honest, he was a man of his word and periodically I was getting financial bonuses which I enjoyed very much. Also, I do not want you to get the wrong idea; we were professionals, not amateurs, and joking around when you have to be serious was not "our thing". But again, the atmosphere at the agency was positive, constructive, encouraging and helpful and to keep it that way we had to pitch out a little joke here and there.

"Sit down Serge," said the director.

I jumped into the chair, across from him, on the other side of the big table with a computer on it and some papers, files and pictures of the director's family.

"How is everything?" asked the director. He was looking at some papers like he was afraid to look directly into my eyes. I even felt some guilt in his behavior. That surprised and puzzled me. I knew that the best way to find the answers to my questions was to wait just a little bit, let the situation develop itself. But a lot of thoughts were going through my head like I had some good computer antivirus program in it searching for viruses. "Did something happen?" "Am I getting a new assignment?" "Did I do something wrong?" "Is it job related?" "Is it personal?" "Is it something else?" And so on and so on and so on.

And I answered: "I am okay, thank you."

If someone looked at me at that moment, they would not see any emotions or panic. I was patiently sitting and waiting for the director to make a move. And he waited as well, taking a pause, probably waiting for me to start asking him questions or he was searching for the right words. Eventually, after the long silence, the director said:

"I need to talk to you about one matter, which is very important, but this is not job related. I need to know what you think and if you have any ideas on how to resolve it. Please let me know if you do not want to get involved..."

The director looked mystified and unsure. This was not his usual confident behavior. And I realized that he is going to talk to me about some personal substance. I was right and wrong. It was personal, but it was personal not to him, it was personal to the director's good friend, to whom he was trying to help. And I said:

"Sir, I trust you and I know you would not ask me to do anything unethical or against the law. We are here to help people and I believe in our line of work be it on the global scale or just in a case of a single individual. If I can help - I will do my best. If I can't – I will try to find someone who can."

The director simply said: "That's what I thought."

Then, this time looking directly at me, he added:

"So, I see. You want to help. In this state of affairs I will provide you with all the information I have. Remember, that matter is confidential, sensitive and not job related. You are asked to do it in your own free time because your work is very important and goes first."

Thinking "we do not have free time at all in our occupation" I was ready to listen to the director with full attention. Now I saw the same professional, strong and smart person in front of me. At this point in our conversation the director was all business and that meant I am going to receive all the possible details, all the keys and clues.

"Before I start," said the director, pulling some notes from a file, which was located on his table, then continued:

"I need to warn you that you might need an assistant to help you with some materials or elements of this unofficial assignment, someone who has knowledge of Psychology and maybe even hypnosis as well. What do you think about our new agent Kristina?"

I answered:

"She is nice, but she is new, I do not know her much and I am not sure if she has the necessary experience yet."

The director looked at me and then added:

"That is how you get the experience Serge. There is a reason she is here and she graduated at the top of her class and her specialization makes Kristina my number one choice, apart from you, for this task. You will understand me in a brief moment, after I tell you everything you need to know."

Thinking "it sounds complicated" I nodded my head saying: "Okay."

"I already talked to Kristina, I did not give her any information yet, just asked if she is willing to help with some investigation in her free time and she expressed the desire to help. I am totally positive we can trust her. I said that you will provide her with all the facts," continued the director.

I called him "Player" in my head because he already figured out my and Kristina's moves and now he was just pulling strings according to his scheming plan. He is good. I do not know my next move myself, but he does, and that is why some of our "community members" call him "The Goblin".

Years ago I learned not to take shortcuts if I do not have to, but in this situation I quickly realized that it is better to invite Kristina here right now, in this case I could see her reactions and I do not have to repeat to her the whole story again. So, I said:

"Maybe we should invite Kristina to join us now, seeing as she is going to be involved anyway?"

The director swiftly calculated something in his mind and then said:

"Okay, give me a second."

Then he dialed on his phone the extension number for Kristina and after she answered invited her to come to his office. A minute later Kristina knocked on the door and asked permission to enter. She was in a good mood (as usual) and she had a pen and a notebook in her hands. Seeing this I thought "I like it, very professional, she is ready to take notes".

The director offered Kristina a seat, next to me, and then said:

"First off, I would like to thank both of you for agreeing to help. I understand that this is not easy, especially considering the fact that you have to do it in your own free time and that it is an unofficial and sensitive matter. I do not have to remind you about confidentiality as well. Both of you are professionals, well, one is a young professional and the other one is very young, but you know what to do and you have what it takes to achieve fantastic results. And moreover, I am sure, you will enjoy working with each other because as I already mentioned – you are professionals."

Even though the director rolled around, not releasing any information so far, I was patiently sitting there and listening to every word said. They teach it at school, that simple and yet powerful rule: "Be patient, patience is a virtue..." And I was a poor student, but I had great teachers and that is why today I do a lot of stuff well enough.

Eventually, the director started his saga. If you are not paranoid or an Intelligence agent, you would not believe everything you have been told or heard and that is good, because any normal person would react like that. And I consider myself an average person, I would not believe the story myself, if it was not director Goldberg himself, who was sitting in front of me and Kristina and giving us information.

ROMEO

Romeo, a twenty three year old young male, a son of an immigrant, came to this country in the year of 1998, when he was just eleven years old. He did not speak any English at all. Since his early years, the age of five, his father, by the way a very good friend of director Goldberg, taught him Martial Arts. And Romeo had the talent for it. By the age of twelve he was already an established fighter, a black belt in Taekwondo and a Champion. He won many competitions and was very promising, practicing hard, spending from two to four and sometimes even five hours in the training facility every day.

Like many other kids in the same situation, Romeo quickly picked up the English language skills and adapted to the local life style. Him and his little sister Ena, she was six years old at that time, went to a nearby public school. At the beginning of their new life Romeo's whole family was doing alright. They initially had some money which they brought from their country of origin and that helped a lot. The father went to a school to study local law to become a legal assistant and the mother went to an English skills program established for immigrants.

About a year later, Romeo's father started noticing a significant change in the behavior of his son and his wife. Romeo begun skipping Martial Arts practices, school, and was caught a couple of times smoking Marijuana. And Marijuana is very dangerous. To explain it in simple words a Marijuana made cigarette contains more cells which cause cancer than the tobacco made cigarette. Also, psychoactive chemicals of Marijuana attach themselves to the fatty components of cells, because Marijuana is fat-soluble and can stay in your body for up to thirty days after use. Alcohol is out of your body in twenty four hours, it is water-soluble. Research indicates that Marijuana has significant impact on memory, heart and lung functions, reproduction and more. And Romeo got the Marijuana from some guy, a neighbor, who was seven years older and already had a criminal record.

Romeo's mother also started acting strangely. A doctor, the family physician, subscribed her some hormonal pills and that, according to Romeo's father's theory, changed her hormonal balance and her love for her husband abruptly disappeared. Suddenly she became irritated, secretive, and angry with him for no reason. The father did not understand why the always healthy woman needed the hormonal pills and felt as though she hates him more and more every day and he was shocked and confused with all of that. Everything happened so quickly and rapidly by the will of some unknown power. Fifteen years of happy life, of marriage, went down the drain like it never happened at all. Being a good observer the father noticed some pattern in everyday events, in Romeo's and his mom's behavior. Some strange people, complete strangers, appeared on a horizon. The father quickly realized that all the events around his family and outsiders involved in these events are the elements of the same chain.

Several people from one of many religious organizations

were working with Romeo. They pretended to help the kid by taking him to an entertainment park for kids, giving him pocket money and so on. The kid asked his father a few times for cash, but difficult times came in and the father did not have a job and could not compete against these people. In reality the kid was brainwashed. Was it just pure theoretical brainwashing or had they used some psychotropic substances was not clear. The kid started acting strangely; sometimes his eyes were open very wide after coming home from entertainment trips. He started saying more and more that the end of the world is coming soon...

Romeo's mother was caught lying as well. She became a cold stranger to her husband. Of course, it is life, different situations do occur, but the father saw the pattern, the certain blueprint, like the whole thing was very well orchestrated. Pretty soon the mother filed for divorce and a few months later the divorce was granted. They went separate ways...

Romeo's father was surrounded with total strangers too. These were well educated people, with good jobs, obviously belonging to a social group of another level and it was not clear at that time why they needed him. He was just an immigrant, who had to take on a lot of low paid employment opportunities in order to try to survive.

While director Goldberg was giving us full details, I had images in my head where Big Boys and Big Girls, meaning adults, were doing awful things to kids, using them for their own good. These people did not care if they ruined someone's life or someone's family; they were deciding the life of others the way they wanted or needed, playing God. And I thought: "Who gave them the right? Who gave them the power? Aren't they afraid that one day their time to answer will come?" I could only imagine the sufferings of the director's friend, when he saw that his family is being ruined and could not do anything about it. Anyway, we are professionals and showing emotions is not for us. But what we could do, we could get additional energy and motivation learning about situations like that.

In a meanwhile, the director continued telling the story, giving us more and more details. These particulars would sound insignificant for anyone who does not care, but for us, trained agents, the more information we get, the better the chances to help and to solve the mystery.

By the age of fifteen Romeo was already an established hooligan and a gang member. There were a number of different gangs in the area at that time. Knowing the fact that Romeo is a good fighter, they used him as a muscle to settle cases. He dropped out of school, stopped practicing Martial Arts, left home and was in and out of police custody very often. The further down the road he moved, the more difficult his situation became. He still periodically saw those people from the religious organization, which were working with him initially, but not as much as before. And his religious views were the same; he kept saying that the end of the world is coming. This continued for a while, until one day he was once again placed into a jail facility on some assault or fighting charges. Spending a few months in a detention center was not a problem for him. He was there before and he knew the drill. This time it was different. At some point, after a few months inside, he called from the penitentiary to his sister and he really scared her by sounding crazy, yelling nonsense and demanding something unknown. Ena could not understand her brother. Not a single thing he said to her, but what she understood is that Romeo is going nuts and he needed help. She called her father and told the story to her mother as well. They could do nothing, Romeo was out of reach. When they visited him in jail, Romeo was just sitting there, behind the glass and not saying anything. Then suddenly he would start shouting something or laugh to himself. Seeing him like that was very scary and extremely painful to his family. While visiting Romeo, Ena used that chance and talked to a correction officer about his mental state and asked if they give him any medication. The CO (correction officer) assured her that they give some meds to Romeo and she should not be worried, Romeo is getting out soon. A couple of days later, someone from the jail called Ena, and said that the CO was mistaken, Romeo is not getting any medication and they did not give him anything at all. Ena was surprised with that answer.

A couple of weeks later Romeo was out, he served his sentence and was a free man now. He came to live with his father. The father, despite the fact that he himself did not have a job, was not getting any assistance and was living in very poor conditions, did everything to help Romeo. The father rented a small room in a basement and had only one bed, which they started sharing with his son. This could not go for long without any conflict. During the night time the father was just sitting on the edge of the bed, praying for his son to get better and Romeo could sleep or he could suddenly become very angry and try to crush anything he saw on his way or could take a shower three times per night and leave at six in the morning to go somewhere.

What was also different this time, after his release from jail, he became a very religious man. And it was not the religion of his family and it was not the religion to which those strangers tried to convert him when he was younger.

It was something else. Now Romeo was carrying holy books with him all the time, he grew a beard and was praying in some foreign, unknown to his father, language. In about a month's time, after Romeo got tired living with his father in that basement, he found a room for himself and moved out.

His sister Ena took him to see different doctors a few times and the doctors were saying that he is okay, just suffers from post traumatic stress and subscribed him some medication.

One day Ena got a phone call from the police. They said that Romeo is in the hospital, he stabbed himself with a knife in his chest, into the heart area, five times...

Ena and her father ran to the hospital right away to see Romeo.

Again, listening to director Goldberg, I thought about how much pain went through the veins of Romeo and his family. Why on earth would a smart and healthy young man try to hurt or kill himself? Just look once more at the word "kill". It does not go along with the word young, no, not in any way. Why? My imagination quickly created the whole frantic picture in front of my eyes: scary, confusing, unthinkable and wrong. Now I understood the directors' desire to help. And I said:

"May I interrupt for a moment Sir; just to clarify some information?"

The director looked at me and made a "go ahead" sign with his arm. Usually, when we have questions, we ask them later, after we receive all the details. This time I decided to ask the question right away, the minute it came to my head:

"Are we allowed to contact Romeo and his father directly, if we need to?"

The director said:

"Thank you. I already thought of that. You are permitted to contact Romeo and whoever else you need, but do not blow your cover and stay discreet. And regarding his father, it will be better for all of us if you do it in an indirect way, through me. I do not want other people to know my agents… Any more questions?"

Both Kristina and I answered: "No", then I added: "Probably later."

The director continued the story.

After Romeo's father saw his son laying on a hospital bed, connected to a number of different machines and sounding devices, and with a tube full of blood stretching out from his chest, it was the last straw for him, he could not bear it anymore. He called director Goldberg right away from the hospital and asked him to meet. They met at some eating place for a cup of coffee and that is how our Boss got acquainted with the story and decided to help. And now two more persons, Kristina and I, are involved.

"Everything is a numbers game", this expression came to my mind at that moment, while I was thinking that a few more individuals (the director, Kristina and I) joined the case and are willing to help. It means that our chances to help Romeo and his family, our chances for success, are growing significantly.

As soon as the director finished with the details, he opened some folder, which was sitting on his table and pulled out a few sheets of paper and some photos from there.

"Here," he said, giving both of us identical documents. "These are the notes, the whole story I already told you, written by Romeo's father. Here is kid's current address, his phone number and these are the photographs of him. Please go through the written materials again to check if I missed anything. And by the way, the kid is still at the hospital, you can see the name of the hospital right there."

I automatically looked at the papers thinking "were do we start?" and said:

"Is there any specific timeframe for the case Sir?"

"No, as I mentioned before it is unofficial, but keep in mind that people are suffering and some other party might be involved. Today, a friend of mine, Romeo's father, sounds paranoid, but who knows what you will discover tomorrow?"

A young and smiling gentleman was looking at me from one of the pictures: blue eyes, a beard, a mustache and a typical haircut of the majority of Martial Arts fighters – short and easy. A kind and confident look on his face plus a characteristic nose of a boxer completed the portrait. I thought that the kid is someone's son and brother, friend and companion, somehow he became confused and lost his identity, but probably he is not guilty and deserves good. On the other photo I recognized the same child, but much younger, perhaps at the age of ten or eleven. He was sitting in a perfect one hundred and eighty degree splits, wearing a uniform, practicing Martial Arts. In the background I saw a miniature angel, a little girl about five years old, his sister. They were happy kids and a happy family.

My thoughts were interrupted by Kristina, who asked the director a question:

"Excuse me, Sir. How far are we allowed to go in our investigation and what available resources can we use?"

It was obvious that the director already thought of that and he said:

"Regarding your professional specialization Kristina, I am talking about Psychology; you can go all the way, all one hundred percent. Regarding the use of your workstations, surveillance equipment and other gear, I would like you to consult with me first; the same goes if you discover something suspicious or unusual, or if you find any urgent and valuable information."

The director paused for a moment, then added:

"Feel free to call me anytime on my mobile phone or just knock on the door here – it is always open for any of our team members. And of course please use your own phones for this investigation. Is it clear?"

I automatically answered: "Yes." Kristina did the same.

The director continued:

"Any more questions?"

We both quickly said: "No."

"Then let me remind you once again that it is an unofficial and sensitive matter, please stay discreet and proceed with caution. And thank you for your willingness to help."

I said: "Sir, do you mind if Kristina and I have a discussion here, in your study, for a brief moment, without any public watching, just to go through some details and ways of communication, figure out our next step, the delegation of responsibilities and so on…"

The director looked at me like sending a "nice try" mental message and then said:

"Why don't you go somewhere after work for a cup of coffee or something, two coworkers, it is not suspicious and you can talk all you need…"

I quickly reacted: "Great idea." And turning to Kristina added: "What do you think? Would you be able to stay late tonight for about twenty minutes?"

"Sure," she answered smiling politely.

"Okay," was my response.

MEAT

When you are investigating something or belong to a very powerful organization, like ours, it does not mean that you are protected and someone is not watching you or not looking into your affairs. No one is immune to it. If you have an interest in a specific organization and you know where this organization is located, which is, most likely, public information, there is a great chance that sooner or later you will find some thread, some way, which might lead you to a bigger discovery. Just start digging and take a look at the nearest eating places first. You will notice that the employees of the company of interest periodically go to these food areas to eat and talk. You can simply sit there next to those people with an innocent face, like a winner of the "Moron of the year Award" and listen to the conversation or use a number of voice recording electronic devices freely available on the market today. I am not, by any means, suggesting to do it, but there is always some method available, in theory and in practice.

Personally, I do not go often to the places close to work to eat or meet with people; I might buy some food there, but will take it away with me and have it at the office.

Being professionals, Kristina and I went to the big shopping mall's food court area to share our thoughts on the case and to create a plan of action, instead of staying close to our place of work. Kristina went to the mall with her boyfriend, who picked her up after work and I jumped into my car, my baby, the Mercedes, which I bought recently. Yes, I can afford it, my pay is good. And this is not the first car of that type, I had one before. Of course you have to service it at an authorized dealer location, they have their own equipment, parts and procedures, but it's worth it, you know that your car would not let you down when you need it the most.

At the mall Kristina's boyfriend, using this opportunity, went shopping and Kristina and I bought some coffee and sat at one of the tables, somewhere in the middle of the food court area. There were not that many people there at that time of day, so we could talk freely, not raising our voices.

Kristina said:

"What do you think?"

Obviously, being new, she asked for my view of the situation. And I answered:

"If our Boss decided to be involved, it is serious. He is almost never wrong; somehow he is able to sense when something fishy is going on. Of course it could be nothing, just the unlucky coincidence of the events, but we have to seriously look into the matter, with all the awareness and consideration. Usually coincidence requires a lot of preparation..."

"I see," agreed Kristina, then added: "But I am sure you thought of something already and know what to do. I am here to help. Please feel free to delegate some responsibilities to me."

"Sure," I assured her, and continued: "The guy is still at the hospital, this could buy us some needed time... Tomorrow, during the lunch hour, we should go pay him a visit. In the morning, at the office, I will print a few business cards for you and for myself, with our phone numbers on it. We are going to be Social Services Workers. This is our legend for the kid and others. In the meanwhile, when you have some extra time, please go through the details of this case and try to write down your thoughts on it. I would like you to focus more on your area of specialization, which is Psychology. Try to throw down a few versions of the events with your views and explanations. And I, in my turn, will go through the matter from every other angle I might find. Then we can compare our notes and analyze the information. Tomorrow's visit to the hospital should also give us something. This is our plan of action for the next couple of days, and as I said already, after we compare our notes and evaluate the received facts we will know what to do next. So, how does this sound?"

"Sounds like a plan," answered Kristina.

We said good bye to each other and went separate ways. Kristina to meet her boyfriend at some store and I, after finishing a cup of coffee, which I was carrying in my hand, jumped into my car and drove away.

I did not go straight to the residence where I live. I went to clear my head at the nearest park instead. With experience and years of service you acquire certain character traits, certain habits, which you follow automatically. Usually I do not go home directly; I drive a little bit around, not much, just to check if someone tails me. And I enjoy driving alone and listening to my favorite music. Basically it is a combination of pleasure with professionalism. This time, walking around at the park would allow me to observe the surroundings, to see anything suspicious and to put my thoughts together. It just started getting dark a little bit, but was still too early, so I parked myself on one of the benches and went through the materials again. Then, while having fresh views and feelings, I wrote them down on a piece of paper. That is what I do. If I have an interesting idea in my head, I write it down and, when some time has passed and I thought it through, I will build on it later.

At home, watching TV, I added a few more sentences to my notes and went to sleep. I knew that the next morning I might add more. Somehow the human brain is still able to work even if a person is asleep. And this is a good practice to sleep a night or two with your thoughts and worries, before you make an important decision.

I woke up at my regular time, did usual stuff: morning exercise, shower, breakfast, trip to the agency, except I came to the office twenty minutes earlier on purpose, to print business cards and to work with my theories. Last night I slept well. During my sleep I saw some unnatural dream, which I wrote down first thing in the morning: I was working on a formula, trying to figure out the proper integers, indexes and coefficients of the value of the committed crime and the appropriate punishment for the wrong doing.

The formula came across like this:

The value of crime = the value of punishment

Or

The value of crime = P E N A L T Y

Where,

P – God's Will coefficient (protected: kids, elders, insane...)

E – the act of God Index (sometimes things happen)

N – the age factor coefficient

A – state of mind

L – circumstances

T – karma Index (previous deeds)

Y – harshness of crime coefficient

= equality symbol (the punishment must be equivalent to the severity of crime)

I would describe the Act of God as an event, which was not planned by the person or persons involved in the happening. For example: someone, while walking on the street, got stung by a bee and that someone, under shock and panic, waved his arms and accidentally hit a passerby.

While working on Romeo's case and going through the chain of the known episodes, some of which looked totally innocent and others really suspicious, not leaving a thing out, I was writing down on a piece of paper my assumptions related to the subject, no matter how foolish they might sound. First I decided to go from simple to more complex and from obvious to conspiracy. And then we need to compare our notes with Kristina. Here is what I had:

- Nothing suspicious or unusual, a natural course of life, not a plot, no third party involvement, no psychoactive drugs, just upset, paranoid and tired of misfortune father is looking for explanations or excuses

- A criminal neighbor acted on his own and was trying to make the kid his customer or a distributor of Marijuana by first offering him Marijuana to smoke and then the kid was supposed to buy it for himself or sell it to other kids

- Someone, for whatever reason, was using the criminal dude, the neighbor, to knock the kid off of his balance, because the neighbor is a neighbor, he is not suspicious, he has the right to be in the area (Who is that someone who has the power over the criminal neighbor?)

- A few people from one of the religious organizations tried to recruit the kid or just share with him their views, these folks were really trying to help in their own way, nothing unusual, except the phrase: "the end of the World is coming...", which got into the kid's head and was often repeated by him

- There are some known incidents when one or another religious organization or sect clandestinely used psychotropic substances to influence its members or prospective members and to deprive these associates of their Will for the purpose of having power over them and to control their actions

- There is still a chance (hypothetically) that religious organization somehow used the criminal neighbor and they worked together to be in command over the kid for whatever purpose they had

- Some other third party used the neighbor and/or religious organization openly or as "blind agents" to screw up the kid and/or his parents: father or mother, or both of them (kids parents – who are they, could they be the reason for kids' suffering?)

- There is a real possibility that for whatever reason some other agency got involved (they are trained agents and have all the resources - proceed with this version with extreme caution)

- Additional possibilities (could be a number of them – keep your mind open)

- A conspiracy theory – some organization picked up the kid to secretly test or use their technology or know-how on him to make the kid some kind of a zombie

I was scared myself of the last paragraph I wrote in creating the possible theories list. I thought of the unthinkable while writing it and kept in my open mind the "what if?" question. The kid came here from some other place. He was a target because of that, because of his origin, and because he is a kid. Kids are future adults and they are the Future. What if you find the way to control a kid today, it means there is a good opportunity that you will have control over an adult tomorrow. Nowadays we know that the employment of hypnosis in combination with psychotropic substances was used many times to manipulate unsuspected people for example in the war conflict zones to increase resistance and support confrontation. We know that mass media such as radio or TV stations and Internet allows to place certain information in the human brain by using the so called 25th frame method which allows to effectively pass the hidden video or acoustic message. Different types of people live in different parts of the world: Black, Hispanic, White, Asians or Natives and we all have brains, blood, bodies and so on. What if you found a substance which is working perfectly let's say on White people? Then all you need is to adjust it slightly to use it on others. This is a weapon. You control someone; you send that someone into the specific region of your choice and then this human weapon will be working for you the way you want. For instance: organizing arguments or forcing Revolutions. I am not a politician, I cannot play with words, but I am sure you see the picture. My mission is to Foresee and Anticipate, Analyze and Improvise, Detect and Protect, gather Intelligence and provide Due Diligence and many, many other things which you could possibly think of. I do not know about the present, but some years ago I remember talking to one immigrant about his desire to get involved and contribute to the community. The gentleman claimed that no matter what he does, he is still not getting any opportunity to be useful. He did the jobs an average person would not even consider doing and eventually that man finished doing research studies. He explained that this is his way to be of use. I recall the gentleman said that he did a number of these Phase one (when they test some medication on humans for the first time after testing it on animals) research studies starting from the ones that involve your brain functions and continuing with everything else. He said: "People like me are just a testing material, a piece of meat, but I do it because I am a good person and my hope is that one day this medication, which was tested on me, will save someone's life…" At that time I did not know if I should believe him or not.

When I was going through the information I had, analyzing every fact, I noticed that we missed, or perhaps it was left out of our view on purpose, maybe by the director or Romeo's father, such an important person in the kids' life: his mother. All we had is that the parents got divorced and that is it. But we need to know, just to clear her out, what is she doing now, what is her background and so on. I made a note to ask the kid, while visiting him at the hospital, about his mother. Also I decided to talk to director Goldberg to get more information on Romeo's father. The more we know, the better, which is contradictory to: the less you know, the better you sleep.

Since early morning and until lunch time, when we had our visit scheduled to see Romeo at the hospital, I worked on my regular duties; very important stuff: preparing a trip to one of the biggest Military/Security/Technology Expositions in the World at one of the European cities. This was a meticulous job, I had to go through a lot of details, analyze many options and possibilities. The time is pressing. We are supposed to leave in a couple of days.

Kristina called on my phone and asked me where we should meet. We agreed to get together outside of the office, not to attract unnecessary attention. The hospital is located just ten minutes away from our building; we should be able to get there quickly.

When I saw Kristina I gave her the notes, which I prepared for this investigation. She did her part too. We decided to walk and to read each other's notes while walking.

Kristina's notes:

The combination of psychotropic medicines and hypnosis could be very effective. Who would use this power on a kid and why?

- To get at kid's parents (by making them nervous – an anxious person is more likely to make a mistake – the idea is to force parents to commit an error – pressuring parents - this would be a job of professionals, but again WHY? And WHO?)
- To manipulate the kid by making him today's, or a future servant (could be a religious organization or some other agency or a party behind the scene)
- Immigration could easily become Cultural Shock not just for a particular kid, but for any human. Today we do not know if any psychoactive drugs and/or hypnosis were used, except for the Marijuana case involving a neighbor
- Something we do not know happened to Romeo

in jail (he was there many times before and he was okay, if you can say so, what happened this time?)

- The unfortunate combination of Cultural Shock and chemical elements in brain (Marijuana, food, other meds) created a confused and vulnerable mind – a good opportunity to brainwash a person under such circumstances
- A possibility that other psychotropic drugs, such as wild plants (for example: Peyote) or organic plants (Psilocybin mushrooms) have been used
- The healthy kid simply became a drug addict or an alcoholic (and the crises had happened)
- Other (we do not have enough information today to make any conclusions)

After we both finished reading our papers I gave Kristina her Social Worker business cards saying:

"You are Ms. Jones now. And I am your coworker Mr. Chic. The names are real. I got them from the Internet. The address on the cards is real too, but with our phone numbers, so pay attention if someone calls you."

"Will do," answered Kristina.

I added: "Of course we are not going to throw these cards away on every corner; we need them just in case… We do not know if those people, whoever they are, or if they exist at all, are still monitoring Romeo. I picked simple and easy to remember names for both of us. You are a young and beautiful lady; you can change your appearance easily. And I am a typical office clerk – it will be hard to describe us if anyone is interested, but our names should be effortlessly remembered by a nurse or anyone else we have talked to. There are also security cameras everywhere and this is good and bad. We can be easily recognized through the security video, this is a bad thing. At the same time if you notice something suspicious or someone is after you; there is a chance that we can trace these followers back using the same cameras and the same security personnel, because they would need to expose themselves to the hospital workers in order to get access to the video. And moreover, we would know – THEY are real. They exist."

The hospital was big in size. We simply approached the information desk and made an inquiry on how to find a patient. Looking tired, but still smiling politely the information desk lady asked us the name of the person we were looking for, checked something on her computer screen and then gave us the directions on how to locate the needed unit. The patient visit hours were from nine in the morning till eight in the evening. Since it was a lunch time, the majority of hospital employees went to eat. Following the directions we easily found the place and saw Romeo resting on a bed. The same young person as we could remember from his picture was looking at us. The only difference was the expression in his eyes, they were opened wide with some sparks of madness or anger in them and his face was really pale. A number of beeping electronic devices were still connected to the Romeo's body. Seeing Kristina and I entering the room, one of the workers behind the monitoring station got off her seat and approached us introducing herself:

"Hi, I am Linda, Romeo's nurse."

"Hi, my name is Mr. Chic and this is Ms. Jones, we are Social Workers to check up on Romeo and see if he needs anything."

Linda quickly and furtively scanned our outfit, remained satisfied and said:

"He is alright for now to talk to, but please make it a short visit altogether, maybe five – ten minutes, okay?"

"Agreed," Kristina assured her.

Then Linda added: "Romeo is a very polite young gentleman. We give him a lot of food, he eats like a machine and still he is hungry all the time…"

We laughed a little bit at the Linda's last statement and then she left the room leaving us with Romeo. He was looking at me and at Kristina in surprise, not saying a word. I decided to break the silence and introduced myself and my partner: "Hi Romeo, my name is Mr. Chic and this is Ms. Jones. How are you? How do you feel today?"

"What do you need?" was the answer. The expression of irritation on his face and the sounds of anger in his voice suggested that we do not have much time here and need to crack the ice quickly.

"I would like to ask you a couple of questions and you can tell me if you need anything, we will see what we can do for you." I specifically started my speech with a pretty straightforward declaration that we need to ask questions to mentally prepare him for this upcoming happening and finished with the pleasant phrase "what we can do for you".

Of course I was not going to ask him anything at that moment, except just to find out what he needs and if we could be useful to him. This was done to establish trust.

Romeo, with his eyes closed, thought for a moment, like he did not hear what was said, then eventually whispered:

"Could you bring me some clean, blank papers, a dictionary and books? I need to write poems and lyrics."

"Of course we can. What books?" was my response.

He slowly moved his arm under the pillow he was laying

on and pulled out a piece of paper with a photograph of a couple of religious books.

I said: "Okay, I will bring it to you tomorrow."

All that time Kristina was standing a little bit aside, letting me talk, doing her job, watching Romeo and his body language. After my last phrase she made me a sign that we have to leave.

I reacted right away: "It was nice meeting you. We have to go now, bye Romeo, see you tomorrow."

And Kristina added:

"Bye Romeo, feel better."

He just looked at us, saying nothing, and closed his eyes. Using this moment I decided to talk to Linda, just to see if we could get anything from her. I approached the monitoring station and said:

"Thank you Linda, we are leaving now. So, how is he? What do you think?"

"He is fine and he is hungry, which is a good sign..." was her response.

"Did anyone come to see him at all?" I continued pushing my luck.

"Yes, I saw his father and his sister, one of them is here every day."

"Anyone else?"

"I do not know. During my shift I did not see anyone. Maybe some other nurse will know more or a doctor. Sorry, I cannot tell you anything else." This last phrase showed me that Linda lost her interest talking to us. I quickly said: "Thanks for your help. Good bye Linda." And we left.

On the way back to our office I asked Kristina the following:

"I need to know your opinion about Romeo and his condition. Do you have any thoughts to share?"

"Sure," answered Kristina and then continued:

"I cannot make any conclusions at this point, we do not have enough details yet, but first impression tells me that Romeo is obviously angry and confused. As I understood he is hungry most of the time and as Linda said this is a good sign. Also he asked for books and mentioned some poetry. And we do not have any information if there was a suicide note. Usually suicide victims leave notes... So, my intuition suggests he is not suicidal, confused yes, but not suicidal. Something horrible had happened to him, but I am sure we can help Romeo to get back on track and live a good life..."

The very next day I returned to the Hospital myself, bringing the requested books, paper to write on and a dictionary for Romeo. I bought all of it, except papers, at the nearest book store. Romeo was half sitting, half laying on his bed, having lunch. Seeing me entering the room made him smile politely. I said:

"Hi Romeo, here are the things you asked for," and I handed the bag with books to him. Then continued: "How do you feel?"

Romeo, happy to see that his request was completed relatively quickly, answered:

"I am okay, could be better..."

I thought that he is still weak, but able to joke around, the progress is apparent. Using this opportunity and his good mood I asked the following:

"Did anyone from your family or friends come to see you?"

Chewing some piece of food he answered:

"Yes, my dad and my sister were here."

"Good, very good. What about your mother? Did she come to see you too?" I had to ask him about his mother just to fill in the information gap we had on her.

Continuing to chew, Romeo answered:

"Yes, she was here the first day, but my parents are divorced and my mom is remarried and now she has three little kids in her new family, so, she cannot come here often."

I decided that it was enough information from Romeo at this point and said:

"I see you are getting better, which is good. I have to go now. I am leaving the city for an indefinite period of time, will be back approximately in a week or so. Do you need anything else?"

He quickly looked at me and answered:

"No, I am fine for now, thank you."

I left. After learning that Romeo's mother remarried again and now they have three little kids to look after, I crossed her out from the "persons of interest" list.

Expo

The day before the departure to Expo all agents from our entire department were gathered in a conference room. We needed once again to go through all the details of the upcoming operation: who does what, in what sequence, when and how it must be done and so on. Just a few of the chosen, including Kristina and I, were actually going directly to the Exhibition, as employees of a company that was participating in the event, using good cover stories. Some more people were supposed to go to the neighboring country, to be able to act quickly, in no time, if their assistance is needed and the rest will stay here to support Intelligence.

Director Goldberg was standing in the center of the room again and again explaining what is expected from each one of us, periodically asking questions, making sure every person understands the importance of the matter and their role in it.

"As you all know our mission is to protect our country and to prevent good things, such as new technological creations for example, from getting into bad hands. Even the best machinery, if used for the wrong purpose, could easily become a disaster..." was saying The Goblin. "And to avert this from happening, we need Intelligence. The access to the show is only available with an official invitation card from the organizer, which gives a good opportunity for the computer hackers to hack into their system and to get all information available. And I am sure they will, they always do. That is why they are hackers. But we cannot do that and we cannot rely on such Intel completely. We need more info than just names and numbers. We need facts, we need faces, and we need a true and real picture of the happening. Past history suggests that not every one of the visitors is willing to use their authentic names and the facial and bodily appearance of a single person could be changed easily. Some stay discreet not to be linked to the event and not to disclose their intentions. It is a huge business opportunity; the global market for Military/Security/Technology is growing steadily and significantly. Thousands of sightseers from all over the World attend the event each year and about one thousand of the exhibitors will be there to present their know-how, sign contracts and make deals. The official delegations from many countries will be in attendance at the show to find the best products for them and to discover the new trends, in which the technology is going. Our specialists will put a good eye on the prospective ideas as well. We know that some others will go even further. Most likely, sometime later, they will announce a tender on supply of certain equipment and the tender requirements often set based on what has been seen at the Expo. They know the winners already before the tender even started and the prerequisites are written for a specific company or equipment. Probably this is called cheating or corruption or double standard. I would like to remind you that we have to do our very best to accomplish our goals. The security at the event is tight, no mistakes are allowed. The greatest Intelligence professionals from top Intelligence organizations will cover the basics at the trade fair. Yes, we have friends and allies and our friends have friends, but we also have some unfriendly organizations who work against us. Please keep that in mind."

While listening to director Goldberg, I noticed that he carefully avoided the word "spies" by vigilantly replacing it with the "Intelligence professionals" phrase. I thought that he is always on his guard, which is a good thing, even if he was making his speech in front of us, his associates and employees.

"We have to be smart with the available resources," continued The Goblin. "Because no matter how much you have; it is always not enough. Also, to cover all the areas which have been planned to cover, plus the unexpected but anticipated ones, is a huge job. So, ladies and gentlemen, do your best, stay focused and help us God! Good luck."

Upon arrival to the Expo, Kristina and I stayed in a hotel sharing rooms with real employees of the company which we represented. Kristina shared her room with Megan Adams and I with Frank DeBure. Megan and Frank were told that we are security professionals, belonging to some private organization, hired by the company to look after the equipment. It seemed to me that Megan and Frank were even glad to have us there, to share the responsibilities which came along with the job. They were simple and polite people, not particularly noisy and I liked that the most about them.

For the past couple of weeks, before the exhibition, we had to learn the products of the company and all the related stuff: the technical characteristics of the devices, how they work, pros and cons and so on. We had to be knowledgeable, quick, trustworthy and proficient. We had to be experts. And let me be honest with you: it is a gigantic job and it was a lot to memorize and understand. It takes years of hard work to become an expert in this field and we only had a few weeks to cover that distance, to make us look like specialists for everyone else, for the few days during the Show. The list of the items included a variety of monocular products, binoculars, scopes, goggles, multi-purpose systems and so on. We represented the best technology available on today's Global market (well, almost the best, we have even more advanced samples already and that is why the decision to sell some know-how was made).

Our technicians, specifically for the trade fair, prepared a few so called multi-purpose devices (systems) by placing in them hidden video and voice recorders. This was done to record everyone interested in the products and to record each passerby, basically to record everything. There was a small unnoticeable switch which would allow to change the regime of work from camera and voice recording to night and thermal vision and back. All we needed to do is to place the devices on the exhibition stand and to periodically secretly replace the memory cards in them. These particular systems had odd numbers on them; this was done for us to distinguish the "loaded equipment" from the similar, unloaded ones. And if someone would want to test out how the system works, we would let them do so by giving them analogs or even the "loaded" ones. Of course, we had regular photo cameras with us too. And we planned to use them a lot, to distract the "mistrustful" individuals as well, despite the fact that sometimes you have to ask permission to use photo equipment.

To summarize and to put everything mentioned above into simple words: the night vision equipment would allow you to see at night or in low light conditions, but if someone is using some kind of a shelter, let's say hiding in bushes or there is a foggy weather, then, most likely, you would not be able to see them. But, if you combine the night vision system with the thermal imaging system, which, by its definition, is able to pick up body temperature, then you will see that someone is hiding somewhere. And this feature is available with real time transmission to a distant receiver. But our technical staff, by the way very smart people (some even call them freaks), when they were making the "loaded gadgets", they decided not to execute the real time transmission feature with the recording devices. This was done for a few reasons and one of them was the tight security of the event. The analysis of the recorded data will be done later and all possible methods, including the face recognition system, might be used.

The three days during which the Exhibition was held passed by very quickly. It was like running a one hundred meters sprint: fast, intense and energy consuming. We did not even have the time to go sightseeing. Every day after breakfast we showed up early at the pavilion to prepare for the huge crowd of people. Visitors from many countries showed their interest in our products and asked us a lot of questions. Thank God that Megan and Frank were there, these professional folks were our face saviors and Kristina did pretty well too, acting naturally. What was interesting; I probably had "an important" face because the majority of people tend to address me with their questions and concerns, even though everyone else was standing nearby. We did an enormous job trying to catch our clients, answering to all possible queries, showing off the equipment, exchanging business information with prospective customers, helping each other and looking after the devices. According to Megan and Frank, who had previous experience participating in similar events, we did pretty well. We were able to secure a big international contract during the Exhibition, plus a few small ones, plus we still had potential clients who were in the process of deciding which way to go and we also needed to verify their background and financial position. Basically participating at the trade fair is equivalent to being on the cover of a magazine. The real and scrupulous job begins after the Show. We had to go through all the information we had, analyzing every fact, including the recordings, and we needed to check the individuals and delegations who came to our booth at the Demonstration, sometimes even three or four times per day to ask questions and to compare the devices, prices and offered services with the competition. We had to make sure that the delegations, the potential buyers of the equipment, are from the dependable countries and our actions are not in violation of the International Traffic in Arms Regulations. Remember, we have to prevent good things from getting into bad hands. And it is no longer a secret that some buy new technology and use it for unlawful purposes or copy it and sell it to others in order to make a profit. And as for those who are undecided, we have our own tools, the so called decision support system, which is specifically designed to help individuals and organizations make the right choices.

Throughout the whole time at the Expo we spent our evenings by resting, eating and drinking well, preparing ourselves for the next day, or, if you say this by using a boxer's terminology: for the next round. I told myself that I have to visit this fabulous city again next time I am on vacation, or when I can use some other opportunity to come and look at the things around here as a tourist.

Surprisingly, everything went smooth. Probably the

rigorous preparation played its part. The only out of the ordinary moment was when one man, acting guiltlessly and using the occasion, came to our booth every single day. He left his fingerprints on all the devices we had. Each time the man asked to show him different products and we were happy to do so. Then the man would play with the gadgets for some time, looking at them at every possible angle, then he would quickly disappear and would show up again later or the next day. We did not follow the guy, knowing the fact that in this massive crowd of people someone might be watching his back, but I made a note to find out more about that "average" person, who did not have a business card to hand out, but expressed so much interest in our commodities. And as I suspected, the "strange" man was one of the employees of a fellow company participating in the event, which had similar, but less popular products.

When the Trade Fair was over, and upon arrival to our home city, the very next day we had another "after the Show" meeting. All the involved and interested parties were present. We needed to go through the achievements and possible mistakes we had at the Expo, set new goals for our staff members, regroup if necessary and once again delegate responsibilities.

To summarize the accomplishments, director Goldberg moved to the center of the conference room in front of everybody and started his speech:

"First of all, I would like to congratulate each member of the Task Force on the successful completion of that stage of the operation, which required some of you to travel abroad. It is too early to make any conclusions yet, but first results suggest that we did a great job and were successful in achieving our goals. We were able not to just actually perform at the highest level possible at the international stage and gather information by spending our taxpayers' money; we in fact gained some capital. Tremendous work ladies and gentlemen, tremendous work! Nevertheless, we still have a lot more to do. I want you once again to go through all the Intel you have, your reports, your notes, I want you to analyze every known and unknown detail and set new priorities. Remember, the main mission now is to keep an eye on doubtful, suspicious, outlaw looking individuals and organizations, who are both on our watch list and not, by closely monitoring them and their actions and to secure potential clients who are uncertain. Please keep your eyes open and your ears clean, as always. Work with your sources and do not forget to periodically motivate those folks. Our people, our assets, is what makes us successful and we have to take good care of them…"

It was obvious to me that The Goblin looked happy and satisfied. Probably the job we did was better than expected and he had some talks with his superiors who told him so. Everyone has a Boss and the game goes at different levels. The Goblin has access to another height and we are a team. It means that the hard work paid off. It also might bring with it some extra bonuses for us, simple agents, since he mentioned that we have to take good care of our people.

Rechecking myself if I forgot any information, I was going through the chain of the past events in my head. No, everything is reproduced in submitted reports and notes. The only worry I had, apart from a number of other worries, is the young gentleman named Romeo, my unofficial assignment. How is he? What is his mental state? Is he getting better? Somehow I liked the guy even though we did not have much chance to get to know each other better.

I decided as soon as we have some recess here at the office we should go and visit him. I was sure that Romeo, based on his last known condition, is still at the hospital. We need to discuss our next step with Kristina and maybe even try to use her specific skills, such as hypnosis or whatever they call it.

The Goblin, for the time being, shifted to the nearest table, took a binder, which he previously left there and pulled some list of paper from it.

"Here," he said, lifting the paper up in the air. Then continued:

"This is the message from…" and instead of saying from whom the note was, he made a gesture with his arm aiming at the ceiling. It was understandable that the letter came from some high profile people somewhere in the country. But I saw something symbolic in his act and thought "it looks like it is the message from God…"

"As I already mentioned," kept saying director Goldberg, "for the past while we were able to achieve significant results in all aspects of our service and hard work is about to bring us something unexpected, but anticipated. We are expanding ladies and gentlemen. The decision was made to give us more resources and flexibility. It means you will see new faces here and we are going to get new equipment, new assignments, new opportunities and such. Most likely some of you will be promoted to new higher positions. Almost certainly every one of us, including myself, will have to go through additional training to upgrade our skills and to learn how to use new gear. As I was told the expansion and reorganization will start shortly. Presumably it will last for a few months. You know when and how to throw in your suggestions or ideas to improve the process, if you have any.

For the meantime please focus on what I said earlier and keep doing a great job".

After the meeting was over I said to Kristina:

"We should visit Romeo tomorrow, during lunch time, what do you think?"

She answered: "I was thinking the same."

I kept going: "If he is better, do you want to try one of your psychosomatic methods on Romeo to get more information about his adventures and such?"

Kristina thought for a moment and responded: "First I need to assess him and see his present condition and if he is ready mentally and physically and everything is okay, then we can try something. The question I have is how to do my work with Romeo when there are so many people around at the hospital. I cannot be interrupted throughout the hypnosis session and we have to stay discreet."

"How much time do you need to work with him?" was my response.

She paused for a moment and said: "The more the better, but I need at least fifteen — twenty minutes, considering the circumstances."

"Okay, I will figure out how to provide you with that much," and I made a baffling face making her laugh, then continued: "so, tomorrow we do the hidden assessment and if everything is okay, the next day or in the near future you will do your magic."

"Be it." mystifyingly whispered Kristina.

Hang on and Be Grateful

The next day, early in the morning, before coming to work, I entered a food store named "Shaw's" and bought a pack of juice and some cookies, chocolates and fruits. I bought it for Romeo. I did not want to visit him empty-handed. Later, at lunch time, as we agreed with Kristina, we went to the hospital to see our patient. Romeo was still in the same room, but the good news was that the "sounding devices and tubes" were disconnected from him and his chest. He was half sitting and half laying on his bed, writing something on a piece of paper. Seeing us coming to visit him, the young man started to smile pleasantly. At the same time as we walked into the room a nurse that was unknown to us quickly appeared from nowhere with the following words: "Hi, I am Romeo's nurse Amanda."

I answered: "Hi, my name is Mr. Chic and this is Ms. Jones, we are Social Workers to check up on Romeo and we brought him some food."

"I have to see it, what is in there?" said Amanda taking the bag with food from me. She swiftly looked inside and returned the bag, then continued: "Romeo is a very well-mannered young gentleman; he is getting better every day. I have other patients to look after. If you need me, I will be there, at the monitoring station."

We thanked Amanda and she disappeared the same way as she appeared a minute earlier.

Romeo handed Kristina the piece of paper he was working on: "This is my latest poem. Do you want to read it?"

"Sure," was the response.

"Could you please read it out loud? So, I will know that you are able to understand my handwriting," and Romeo made himself more comfortable on the bed, ready to listen.

Kristina started to narrate. Here is exactly what was written in the paper. Romeo insisted we take it with us.

Romeo's poem

No liquor, no weed
Was the path to succeed
In a World full of bustas,
Hustlers, ballers and greed.
Glad I can read
On the daily go over my psalms
And my Quran, praise Allah,
Plant a seed.
God bless the veterans
That lead in this life
Gotta hussle at light speed,
Good and bad deeds
Stay fully equipped with God's power
And strengths, make progress
And treat yourself to the purest of Faith.
Help those in need, honesty is a trait
You can't cheat, a pure breed
On the road to Zion success guaranteed.

Keep your relatives close and your neighbors indeed
Water my garden till ain't got no more weeds.
Bet you the forbidden trees
Was them apples and weed.
Old school and clean is the way to succeed
Pray seven times a day
Till we purified clean.
When I am old I'm trying to kick back
Watch TV with my kids.
Keep your library jam packed
With materials to read
Let knowledge feed the hunger that breeds.
It ain't no game
Can't get through the heavens gates with no key
Audhu bi-llahi mina shaitani rajim
Bismillahir Rahmanir Rahim
La haula wala quwatta illa bi-llahi-l
`Aliyu-l `Azim
Please say it from within
Heart, soul and mind might be what triggers the sin
Please learn a trade or a skill
Living in this workaholics' world that we in.
Allah moves the clouds and the wind
With love and raw power
Showers the soil and clears of our sin
Islam is the religion we gotta give in.
Two sides to the world, the righteous shall win
Please do not judge by the color of skin
God helps the situations we get in,
But do not test Him
Suggestions from the right and left twin
Listen to intuition, choose right over wrong

Time will be gone, stay in on track
Paying mind to the nature
And this powerful songs.
Other words – meditation, realization
Mentally patient, shall overcome the ignorant
Go down Islam nation, keep your hope alive
Receive blessings, rare sightings of Angels
Got me impatient, keep your hope alive
And never let that eternal fire die down
To God I bow down forever he blesses
For ever rocking that crown
I forever bow down in prostration
Life deep, feel the inspiration
Keep your path pure, study hard
Be strong and patient
Walk with God to achieve your destination
If you really want success
Can't give in to no temptation
Get strong, face life with dedication
Purify your heart, soul and mind
With the best of meditation
We are under God's watch
So, do your best in any situation
Through the struggles, through the storms
Hang on and be grateful

When Kristina finished reading the poem saying: "It is really nice and inspirational, did you write it yourself?" I realized that I still had the bag with food in my hand and hurriedly handed it to Romeo, saying:

"This is for you, some fruits, chocolates…"

He took the bag, said: "Thank you" and "Yes, I wrote it". Then he placed the bag on the table by his bed.

At that very moment, with a look of surprise, a youthful and beautiful creature entered the room. It was Romeo's sister Ena. You could see the relationship between them right away. Ena had another bag with food in her hands. I thought "they, the family, love their son and brother, this is good; he has some support". Ena made a fist and greeted Romeo in a certain way, like it was their tradition or something and then she quickly kissed him on the cheek. Ena's bag with food landed on the same table as the previous one. Probably Romeo was not hungry or maybe he was shy. I decided to take initiative and said: "You must be Romeo's sister?"

She answered: "Yes, I am. My name is Ena." It was invitation enough to release our names and I proudly declared: "My name is Mr. Chic and this is Ms. Jones, we are Social Workers to check up on Romeo's condition." Then added: "Nice to meet you." Kristina did the same.

Ena replied: "Nice to meet you too." I made "it's all yours" sign to my partner and addressed to Romeo's sister: "May I talk to you in private for a brief moment?"

She just nodded her head like saying "yes" and we left the room heading to the distant corner of the corridor, away from the area and monitoring station.

I said: "I want to talk to you about your brother, is it okay?"

"Sure, if you want to help him," was her response.

"Why would you say that? Was anyone trying to hurt him?"

Ena answered: "I do not know, but my brother is here

and this is not good. He is not supposed to be here at all, especially with that diagnosis."

I reacted: "What is his diagnosis?"

"I do not know; I am not a doctor. All I know is he has some mental problems, he never had before, and now those physical injuries," was her response.

Suddenly Romeo with an angry voice yelled from his bed: "Stop talking about me. I hear you."

Ena whispered: "His hearing, as well as his other senses, is extremely good now. We shall move further down the passageway from this spot. I do not want him to get upset."

I said: "I see. Let's do it." We saw some kind of a common area with chairs and tables inside and decided to go in there.

I continued with questions: "Did you have a chance to talk to a doctor or a nurse at all about Romeo's condition?"

For a moment Ena looked puzzled, then answered: "I am here almost every day and each time you ask a nurse or a doctor about any patient, they do not tell you anything. All they say is that it is a privacy issue and they are not allowed to discuss any details without permission from the patient. And my brother does not want others to know whatever thing they might tell us. But he is getting better day after day, I mean physically. I can see it."

Listening to Ena, I felt her worries for her brother. Obviously she loves him and she is very smart. In the meantime Ena continued: "The doctor said Romeo will be out of the hospital in a week or so, but me and my father, we think he needs some psychological help. This department is for physical injures only. To get assistance with his mental condition he must be seen by some other doctor. I think they scheduled the meeting already, I mean the doctor from the other department is supposed to come here soon and do an assessment."

I said: "Interesting. Actually all of it makes sense. I am not talking about the privacy issue here; I am talking about the treatment. It could be dangerous to mix different medications. First they cure his physical injuries and after he is good, they will start working on his mental matter."

"I agree with this strategy and disagree," Ena kept defending her point of view. "Safety must be first, I agree. But disagree, because they are just going to prescribe him some pills, which he is supposed to take every day and have periodical visits to the doctor's office for a check up, meaning staying on his own. And this is dangerous. You know what happened to him and why he is here, he needs twenty four hours observation. At the hospital it is a sure thing, out there, when he is by himself; it is unpredictable. We tried to talk to the doctors to convince them to keep Romeo at the hospital longer, until he really gets better, but they say they cannot force him to stay if he does not want to. And my question is: how could you leave it up to a mentally unstable person to decide what's best for them? To me the answer is obvious."

You can't argue with logic and I asked the next question: "So, if this is the case, what do you plan to do to help your brother?"

Ena again thought for a moment, then answered: "We will keep looking for all possible help, from doctors, nurses and others; basically from anyone who is able to lend a hand or knows how to do it. And when Romeo is out of here we will be monitoring him more closely. We need to stay positive and show him love and support. He must know he is not alone."

The time passed by very quickly. It's already been fifteen minutes since I started the conversation with Ena. In my understanding, Kristina had a really good chance to do the initial assessment on Romeo and I said to his sister: "Thank you Ena, you were helpful. We can go back now. I do not want to take away the time you planned to spend with your brother."

Still smiling politely Ena replied: "No problem."

When we got back to Romeo's temporary place of residence, we saw Kristina standing in front of him looking directly into his eyes. Romeo seemed to be calm and thoughtful. Noticing us approaching the room Kristina said: "You did a great job young man. We have to leave now, but I would recommend you to practice this psychosomatic exercise we just did to activate your internal strength and to make your energy work. You will feel much better."

Then she looked at me like transmitting a message "we can leave, everything is good here" and said: "We have to go. It was nice reading your poem and talking to you Romeo, see you tomorrow. Bye. Bye Ena."

I thanked Ena for her help and addressed her brother: "Get better Mister, you have a long and beautiful life in front of you. Remember everyone is unique and your poem is powerful. Thank you for allowing us to read it. Bye. See you tomorrow."

Romeo and Ena both replied "Bye" and we left. On the street, going back to work, I asked Kristina if she had a chance to evaluate Romeo's present physical and mental state and was really surprised with the answer. Kristina patiently, and in simple words, explained to me her opinion about the situation with our patient and what we should do to help. Here is her speech: "I noticed something interesting.

Romeo is easy to work with. Today I did not have much time to figure out the reason for it and I do not know yet if this is due to his natural abilities or because of the medication he takes. It is also possible that someone, some psychologist or hypnotizer, previously worked with him and implanted the phony recollections into his confused mind during hypnosis sessions. The danger is – we do not know how the kid was programmed, if he was, and for what purpose. Most likely it will be difficult to retrieve the information from Romeo's mind because obviously these pseudo practitioners have extensive experience in manipulating other people. First, they create a vulnerable mind in the head of a targeted individual and then, the so called "subjects" are led to believe that they hear God's voice. They think God talks to them directly and gives orders. The "subjects" are brainwashed to forget the hypnosis sessions and sometimes they act totally normal or on the opposite consider themselves "chosen". Every now and then these poor people feel free and independent, but they are not. It is an illusion and it is an imprisonment. For me the question is: "How can we help Romeo, this particular young man and his family?" And I have an answer. We will try to determine the reason for his recent behavior, see what led to this accident and if some other party was involved. Based on my one on one experience with him today, I am sure I will be able to pull out something. After that, when we have more data to work with, we will decide which is the best way to help."

I was carefully listening to my partner, not interrupting her. I did not want Kristina to lose her thoughts, while answering my questions, because she is still under the certain impression of visiting Romeo at the hospital.

Addressing me Kristina said: "Tomorrow is a good day

to continue what we started today. Do you think you will be able to remove everyone from the area, including visitors and employees and let me do a session with our patient?"

This was a difficult question. How could you remove, for example floor workers or nurses, from the area in which they have a duty to carry out? And I answered: "We will see. There is always a way to do something if you look deep into the matter and prepare yourself scrupulously."

Kristina just replied: "Okay, pull your magic and help us God."

The next day, early in the morning, before coming to work, I again went to the local store and bought some food for Romeo. Then, at work, I did some quick research on psychiatric medication and made some valuable notes, which I was going to use later. When, at lunch time, Kristina and I showed up on Romeo's floor at the hospital, there were just a few people at the monitoring station: walking, sitting, talking and doing something. One of them was a familiar face, Romeo's nurse Amanda. Seeing us she smiled politely, like we knew each other very well already, and then made a demand to show her what was in the bag. Kristina, who held the bag, because I gave it to her earlier, with the same polite smile said: "Oh, it is just some food for our big man." Amanda quickly looked inside the bag and returned it without saying a word. Not wasting any time Kristina, according to our plan, went straight into the room to work with Romeo. I pulled a piece of paper out of my pocket and with an innocent face, quite loudly, to get everyone's attention, addressed to Amanda: "I am sorry Amanda, do you know what Nitrazepam is? I think it is some kind of medication."

I noticed that my trick worked. I got everyone's

attention. Medical professionals can't resist showing off their "knowledge of the profession" when they hear some "uneducated" talks about medicine around them. Amanda, suspiciously looking at me, answered: "Yes it is." Then added: "It is hypnotic stuff used for treating mental disorders." She was looking directly into my eyes like asking "why do you need to know it?" and I, playing my role, explained: "I am doing some research at work. This is on the United Nations treaty on Psychotropic substances, which was signed in 1971. This treaty was designed to control psychoactive drugs such as psychedelics, amphetamines, barbiturates and so on. I do not know much, but I understand that every now and again new drugs are being discovered and used for unlawful purposes causing a lot of harm to society, especially to young people. But the Convention allows only medical and scientific use of the drugs..."

Suddenly the man, sitting in front of the computer screen nearby at the monitoring station, said: "Another name for this medication is Mogadon. Somehow most of these substances have second names, for example: Diazepam and Valium. It is the same medication, but different names."

I gratefully looked at the gentleman to encourage him to participate in the discussion and continued: "I have a big list of various names of the medicines here, which I have to find out about. And you know what is really sad regarding all of this, some countries, even those with a good reputation on the international stage; refuse to comply with the Convention's requirements to control the movement of psychotropic substances inside these countries and across their borders."

Talking to Amanda and to the gentleman sitting by the computer, I kept in mind the time frame needed for

Kristina to work with Romeo and at the same time I was furtively screening the surrounding area, trying to get everyone involved in the conversation and keep them away from the room where the hypnosis session was held. The man was probably "in the mood" to talk because he asked me: "What are the other names you need to know about?"

I answered: "I have it right here, but if you don't mind, may I ask you first about the difference between the so called potent hypnotic and the hypnotic agent. And why are they different?"

The man thought for a moment, then said: "One is stronger than the other. For example: Triazolam is a potent hypnotic, while Temazepam is a hypnotic agent, brand name Restoril, a drug which induces sleep. Psychiatric medications are not our area of expertise here, in this department. If you need to know more, in exact details, you should talk to a doctor whose specialization is mental disorders."

I did not want to "lose" the guy and quickly said: "Oh, no, you are very helpful, you know so much." The gentleman proudly replied: "That is why we go to school for so many years..."

We laughed together. Amanda and some other lady, who was in the area too, joined us in our amusement. I continued: "I really appreciate your help and apologize for the many questions that I ask. It is so confusing, all those "zepam" endings: Diazepam, Temazepam, Lorazepam... You medically professional people are amazing. You know a lot and you help others. I have so much respect for your profession."

The other lady, which was sitting next to the gentleman and doing something, quickly reacted: "I wish everyone could say that, especially the decision makers. If they could have a little more respect for us, we would have better working conditions, better pay and so on. We do our very best to help people and sometimes we need help ourselves, but it seems like no one sees it..."

Some employees and other unknown individuals were passing by here and there, entering rooms, doing something. I realized that I had stepped on the sorrow callus of these great medical professionals and if I did not stop them by changing the topic, they would all join in the conversation. And who knows? Maybe I will have at least five or ten extra minutes which I need desperately. At that moment, Amanda suddenly got up and, luckily for me, went in the opposite direction from Romeo's room. I kept my position in the area for a few more minutes agreeing with the lady on unresolved issues, looking into her eyes and periodically saying: "I see or I understand". And eventually I thanked the gentleman for his help, wished the sensitive lady Gook Luck and left. I did not go inside the room yet where Kristina and Romeo were, I just parked myself near the entrance. The door, made of glass, was closed. In the room, the wall facing the hallway was made of glass as well so that you could see inside. I saw Romeo half sitting, half laying on the bed, as usual, like he was sleeping or something and Kristina, next to him, doing her magic. I did not want to interrupt or distract them and moved further down the corridor, but still stayed visible for Kristina and still close to the entrance door in case if someone decided to go in. I had to protect it. In about fifteen minutes time Kristina called me into the room to say "Hi" to Romeo. He had that "just woke up" expression on his face, but did not look angry. On the opposite, he was in an excellent frame of mind. After I greeted him, Romeo said: "I saw an Angel. Right here. She talked to me."

"Really?" I honestly showed my interest and excitement. "What did she say?"

"We just talked," was Romeo's response. "She asked me questions about "How I feel" and stuff. Do you believe me?"

I assured him: "Of course I believe you. And to tell you more – this is a good sign. You will get better. Your life situation will change soon too. You are a good young man and deserve the best."

"I agree," jumped in Kristina.

"And I agree," said Amanda, entering the room. Then she continued: "How is everything here?"

"We were leaving already. We see Romeo gets better each day. You guys do a great job fixing him," answered Kristina. I quickly reacted to Kristina's "we were leaving words" and said: "Bye Romeo, bye Amanda and thank you."

Amanda replied: "Bye," and then added: "He is out of here soon. The doctor said our job with him is almost done. We will keep Romeo in our unit for a few more days just to make sure he is okay and then he is on his own." Seeing a look of surprise on my face Amanda quickly added: "Or maybe the doctor will decide to transfer him to some other department, I don't know."

We left. On the way back to work Kristina said: "Thank you for giving me the time I needed to work with Romeo. I think I got something. Do you mind if I explain my findings to both you and director Goldberg at the same time so as not to repeat myself?"

I answered: "Sure, this makes sense."

At the end of the day, about twenty minutes before leaving work, The Goblin, Kristina and I met at director Goldberg's study to discuss the situation and to figure out our next move. The Goblin, as the leader of the group, started his speech first:

"I see you people do a great job with your regular duties and with the unofficial investigation. Thank you. As I understood you have news to share. I have new information too. I was not just relying on your hard work; I did some digging as well. I asked a friend of mine, Romeo's father, to help. He was more than happy to do so. Also, I asked our sketch artist Jessica to lend a hand. Do you remember the details about Romeo's family and the time when his father was surrounded by total strangers belonging to a social group of another level? And then suddenly these people surrounding the father disappeared into nowhere, the same way as they appeared on his horizon unexpectedly... So, just in case, I asked Romeo's father to provide us with the description of these folks and Jessica drew a few sketches of these individuals. I ran the images through our database and, as you probably figured out already, we got a match. One man was identified. He is a restaurant owner in downtown. As soon as I knew that this man operates a restaurant, right away I decided to check what we have on him and his contacts. Restaurants are often used as tools to gather Intel or conduct some other activities, and this is done not just by organizations like ours, but also by criminals, business people and some others who do it too. It is a public place, easy to get in, lots of people, big crowds. Also, it is not difficult to convince the restaurant's owner to cooperate. Because if they do not, then there is a chance that some client will accidentally find a fly in a soup or a cockroach in a salad while eating their food in there with an old friend, who turns out to be a local news reporter. I am not going to lecture you on this topic, you know it already. I am just providing you with new information. So, after checking the circle of the possible contacts of that restaurant owner, I found a link to a gentleman named Nick Lavender. Nick is with the "SSSS" agency. He is probably a curator of that restaurant owner and his companions. The "SSSS" agency has a butcher's reputation. And to me, knowing the fact that this guy Nick is involved is already a sign that others might be agents too, or the man could use them as "blind agents". Just in case, I showed a photo of Nick to Romeo's father and he recognized the guy. He saw him a few times on different occasions…"

En Passant

Listening to director Goldberg, I thought that we should thank him for his help. New information often leads to new development. Also, I wanted to hear Kristina's findings; she looked like she was somewhere else, probably in her memory, watching Romeo in his endeavors. In the meanwhile The Goblin continued:

"Now we know that someone else was involved and knowing particular facts about that someone, I have to make a conclusion: there is a little game going on. We do not know yet who the other players are, we do not know the rules and the purpose of the game and why this family was involved in it. But we are diggers and we want to succeed. We will find the answers. So far it looks like Mr. Nick and company decided to use Romeo in some scheme they long planned and this plan involves religion. Maybe they want to infiltrate the kid in some organization as their secret agent and to force parents, whose religion is different, to support their son's "decisions". For example: if you look at the stabbing incident under a different angle, then you might see that everything is scary: a knife, injuries, a lot of blood, friends turned their backs on him, no one wants to deal with a crazy person. But actually there was almost no damage. The kid is now healthy and mentally stronger, and he is out of the hospital soon. Now his family will support his new religion: whatever he wants; anything, they just want him to be healthy and happy..."

Then The Goblin turned to Kristina and said: "I feel, Kristina, as though you have something to share? Please go ahead. I have finished."

My partner, looking periodically at me and at the director, like she was searching in her beautiful head for the right words to make it easier for us to understand, came up with the following: "It is clear to me now, after my partially successful effort with Romeo, that someone else had previously worked with him too. And that someone has skills. They implanted whatever they wanted into his brain, and after that tried to clean up all the possible traces in his mind, which could lead us or some other professionals, to them. Anyway, using one of the known methods, I was able to retrieve some information out of Romeo and so far I do not like what I found. I will tell you about my discoveries in a minute, but first I would like to point out that I need some more time with the patient, I need better working conditions, not like at the hospital, where at any given moment the hypnosis session might get interrupted and I am asking you Sir," then she looked at The Goblin and continued: "to authorize the use of psychotropic substances on our subject in order to achieve better results. It is a necessity. We are dealing with skilled people here who are almost certainly well equipped and will stop at nothing."

Director Goldberg scratched his head, probably thinking about Kristina's proposition and then answered: "According to the information I have, the kid is out of the hospital soon. This means we can arrange a good opportunity for you Kristina to work with him at one of our safe houses, or anywhere else. This is not a problem. Regarding your second request, I say yes, use whatever you think is appropriate, but keep things under strict control and play it safe."

Kristina said: "Got it. Thank you Sir."

While Kristina and director Goldberg, my coworkers, had their conversation, I thought that this case is not as simple as it appeared to be initially. Obviously, someone is after something, but so far all we have is questions: "why that particular kid?", "why that particular family?", "who is behind all of it?" and so on.

In the meantime Kristina continued: "I tried to work with Romeo backwards, starting from his last known event and his injuries. The kid lives at some residence, where he rents a room. There is also another man, at that residence, around thirty years old, who rents the neighboring room and the house owner, a middle aged lady, lives at that house as well. The lady, the house owner, lives on the ground floor and the men live on the second floor. When Romeo stabbed himself in the chest, everyone was at the house. Before it happened, Romeo saw his neighbor smoking marijuana. It is not clear yet if the neighbor offered Romeo to share a cigarette with him or if Romeo asked the neighbor himself. Another question is what triggered the stabbing event. Maybe it was Romeo's depression; maybe he had some alcohol in his system and the combination of alcohol with marijuana and depression led to the happening. Another possibility, we have to keep our eyes open, is that Romeo was programmed for this event by those unknown people and the lady or the man could pass "the activation code" onto him, to force him to act. This coincides with your version Sir," and Kristina looked at The Goblin, then continued: "A lot of blood, everything is scary, parents in shock, but not much damage done. The hypnosis session with Romeo revealed that he, after he started smoking marijuana, does not remember a thing, only a huge and scary storm in his head. Then later, when he was laying in his room with a knife in his chest, he clearly remembers the lady, the house owner, entering into his room, acting unusually calm for an event like that, and taking pictures of everything with a photo camera. The lady called the ambulance, the paramedics came and took him to the nearest hospital where Romeo was admitted, from which he was transferred to another hospital, where he is now. He does not remember seeing the marijuana man after smoking a cigarette, but he remembers everything else starting from the "photo camera" moment. At the time of the stabbing Romeo was out of prison for a few months already. Nothing significant happened during these few months, except the fact that somehow he clearly remembers his meetings with his new probation officer, a gentleman named Norton and a counselor lady named Sharon. Before today, analyzing all the information I had, I couldn't put Romeo's accident and these two people together, but after taking into consideration our new leads and the new name Nick Lavender provided by the director, I tend to believe now that these "insignificant" details or mentioned persons, could belong to the same chain. Anyway, let me get back to my hypnosis session with Romeo. At the beginning of serving his time, he had a roommate and that roommate happened to be a religious person. They talked about religion a lot and Romeo started noticing that he "feels funny" after eating the available food and drinking certain liquids. Probably he was drugged and brainwashed. And with the "funny feelings" different visions and hallucinations came in. He saw angels, he saw God, paradise and so on. He started hearing voices... Romeo recalls that at some point, while still being in prison, he was punished for nothing and placed into isolation: a tiny, tiny dark cell by himself, with no one else. That was a really bad experience for him. He felt like something, like some energy waves are coming from a nearby place and that those waves do him harm. He claims that he felt like some remote equipment or devices in the neighboring room were aimed at him, like someone conducted a distant experiment using him as the subject."

Kristina stopped for a brief moment to catch her breath, and then carried on: "Of course, I did not have much time to work with Romeo and I did my best to extract those pieces of information out of him. Nothing major so far, not any real facts, but I am sure I will be able to break that wall and find what we are looking for. If something awful was done to the kid, we will uncover the truth."

I felt it was my time to speak and as soon as Kristina stopped, I said: "I am aware that in some countries certain people perform experiments on prisoners, this is like permission "to do whatever you want" for them because no one can prove anything and they, these fanatic people, will not be punished for their deeds and can always blame the "subject", saying that the particular individual could not tolerate the environment of the prison and went crazy. But when you hear about similar occurrences somewhere close to the area you live in, you do not want to believe it."

Director Goldberg, The Goblin, looked at me and broke in with the following: "You are not naïve Serge, I know it. I understand your doubt. The question is: Can they do that? By they - I mean those people, most likely well educated individuals, with an "unusual" mind set. And my answer to you will be - Yes. If they can communicate a deadly virus, a lethal disease, into the body of a healthy living person, a real human being, whom they first had to find, brainwash and make a zombie out of... and then send this infected person to a country of their choice, intending to spread out deadly viruses, causing death to innocent people, then yes, they sure could do such a "simple thing"."

Kristina and I were both silent for a moment, listening to the director, when The Goblin suddenly asked me: "Do you play Chess, Serge?"

Not knowing "his angle" and where The Goblin is going with this "Chess question" I cautiously answered: "Yes, sometimes, a little bit."

The Goblin continued: "Then most likely you know the so called special "En Passant" rule. But anyway, let me remind you. I think that the "En Passant" term is French for "in passing". For example: when a pawn makes a double step from the second row to the fourth row, like its trying to sneak past the enemy pawn, which is already located at the adjacent square on the fourth row, by taking two steps instead of one, then this rival pawn, in its next move, may move diagonally to the square that was passed over by the double stepping pawn, which is, as you can see, now on the third row. And in this same diagonal move, the double stepping pawn is taken. This taking of the pawn must be done right away. If the player who has the ability to take that pawn does not do this in his first move after the double step and decides to make a different move, then the player loses his or her right to make the capture. The move must be made immediately or not at all. If you come across a similar situation in a game, you should think carefully. Do not make the capture because you can. Make sure that the move is the right one for you. You can make the move or not. And here is the catch. It is your decision, you are the "Player", and you are the "Boss". You can do your "En Passant" move or you can just do something else, make some other move. And to transfer this Chess rule into the matter we are dealing with, these people, those fanatics, they have the advantage: they have only one rule – they can always make a move. See the difference? In Chess the "En Passant" move must be made immediately or not at all. In real life, these fanatics make their own rules. They can make any moves whenever they want. They do not see a single person; they do not care if that person gets hurt or if that person has a family. They see things differently and work with a different scale. These people could easily sacrifice their lives and the lives of others in the name of science or for some other purpose they believe in. I am not sure if we can change the mindset of these people or the system in which they work, but obviously we can try to save Romeo, this particular young individual, who happens to be in a difficult situation. I am sure you are agreeing with me. Also I would like to ask you to think of other ways to help him. You met Romeo a few times already and probably noticed some character traits, some interests or hobbies he has. As soon as we get Romeo involved in something useful and positive, maybe even into some interesting program to learn new skills, then the better the chance we have to help him."

Kristina decided to share her findings right away: "I noticed Romeo has a very good memory. He writes poems, lyrics and some of them are very long, but he remembers every single word and every single line. And in addition to that, I think he likes computers and electronic devices. When I worked with him he also said that he is going to get his driver's license. So, obviously with a little help, he can get back on track and be a happy and successful young man."

I jumped in: "Kristina is right and as I recall Romeo is a black belt in Taekwondo and he was a Champion. This is good, especially if we give him proper training and as I recollect we are expanding..." I looked at director Goldberg to see his reaction. He seemed to be thinking of something; maybe he was considering what Kristina and I just said. I continued: "Sir, do you think we might have some opening, some internship position or something to help the kid?"

The Goblin answered: "Good idea people. You always want to have someone who really can fight in your team. But first we need to wait to see what Romeo's doctors are going to say. As I understood he is getting out of the hospital soon and this means that physically the kid is fine. I need to know his mental condition. I need to know what those psychologists say, and what their diagnosis is. And I suggest you Kristina do your own independent assessment or a second opinion or whatever it is called. Either way if the kid is healthy or crazy, we are going to help him. If, in the best case scenario, the kid is healthy, we can bring him in directly and make him a trainee or something. If the kid is crazy, we need to know to what degree and still we will try to help. And if, considering the worst case scenario, the kid is actually sick, then we will help him get the papers stating that he is unwell and emotionally unstable... and it could still work for us and for him. There are a number of jobs out there where a person with such papers might be of use and as you both know: you cannot prosecute the mentally unfit..."

I thought: "That is why The Goblin is The Goblin. He is able to think. Right away he saw the situation with Romeo totally through and figured out different ways for how the agency could use the kid. We are all adults here and we are all professionals. And we all clearly understood what the director meant when he mentioned medical papers. A person, with such documental proof that they are crazy, could do anything, almost anything with no legal responsibilities at all…"

Kristina probably thought the same because she looked sympathetic and concerned. After a brief pause she said: "Life is life, we will do our best and we hope for the best and yet we are prepared for anything…"

Seeing our understanding director Goldberg said: "I feel some philosophy and some sensitivity in both of you, this is good. Whatever life throws at us, we are still human and we have to act accordingly. I am sure everything will be fine. I think our meeting is over now, do you have any questions?"

We did not have questions at that moment. The Goblin, showing respect, went to open the door himself for us saying: "Let me once again express my gratitude to both of you for your honest help. I appreciate it."

Both Kristina and I thanked the director in return and we left.

It's Complicated

The next day I was busy with my work when director Goldberg called me into his office again. Usually in situations like that, even if you are prepared for anything or almost anything, something still keeps nagging you inside: what is it regarding? But I quickly forced myself to stop guessing because I had about seven projects on which I was already working. This meeting could be about any one of them or about something else. What difference does it make for me? I still have to do my work. This time The Goblin went straight to business. He said:

"Serge, for the next while, you have been assigned to a special task team and you have to report to this person at the specified location today." The Goblin handed me a piece of paper with some information on it, then continued:

"Pick up your emergency kit and go right away. It is urgent. And do not worry about your current projects, you can return to them later. Also, I will see what I can do to help."

Not showing any emotions at all I asked the director: "I understand, I am leaving now, but could you please provide me with more information, briefly?"

Director Goldberg answered: "Just a few minutes ago I got a phone call from that person; you see his name on the instructions paper I gave you. Let's call him Mr. X.

And Mr. X. specifically asked for you. There has been some leakage of important information somewhere and they, the officials, the people in charge, are forming a team now to fix the problem. As I was told, agents from different agencies, including the military, will be working together on this case. If you ask for my opinion, what do I think about the situation, I will give you an honest answer; I do not like it. And I do not like when my agents work for someone else. Also I do not believe the "official" version of the event given to me. It is always like that: when you have a joint operation and different agencies are involved, wait for something really complicated… That is all I can tell you for now. Go; pick up your things and good luck."

I thanked The Goblin and went straight to my desk. After I checked if everything is in order, I left the building quickly. I knew I had to hurry up. The seriousness of the matter was written on the director's face. On the way to the place of my new assignment I dialed Kristina's number. When she picked up I said: "Hi Kristina, it is Serge. How are you?"

Kristina answered: "Hi there, I am fine. How are you? Can I help you with something?"

I briefly explained: "Sorry, I did not have a chance to talk to you at the office, had to leave quickly. I am going to be working at some other place for a while, this is directors' order. Just wanted to inform you about that, and wanted to ask if you think you could work on our project with Romeo by yourself for now?"

"Sure," was Kristina's response, then she continued: "Romeo is a nice young man and there are still a few more days before he is out of the hospital. Do not worry, I will figure something out."

I thanked Kristina. We agreed to call each other periodically for updates and to see how the situation develops.

Upon arrival to the specified address, I was surprised to discover that the place had very tight security. It gave you a strange feeling, like some famous RAP singer or an actor was visiting the building at that time. Sometimes these Celebrities have more security personnel then the President himself. They can afford it. But one might argue that the President's boys and girls are better trained and more skilled and so on... And I am not arguing, just saying...

With a very serious face the security guard asked to see some identification papers. After learning my name and checking something in his notes, he quickly, but paying full attention, went through my belongings and politely asked me to follow the signs and go to section "C" on the second floor. While I was picking up my stuff the guard called someone on the phone and informed them about my arrival.

Section "C" was like a little hotel with a common area, it had a big TV, and included a number of separate rooms, fitting two people each. Also there was a kitchen, a sports facility and so on. As I understood, the door to the sector was locked all the time and you needed some card or a pass to go in or out. Also, there was some kind of a monitoring station or something where the person on duty was present all the time. When I entered the place, two guys, one of them in a military uniform, and two ladies, were already in the common area, sitting, sipping juice or whatever it was and watching TV. I recognized a familiar face – an agent from some other Governmental agency. We had a chance to work together on a case a few years ago. His name was John

Kalger. Seeing me entering the area John said: "Hi Serge, long time no see. How are you?"

I answered: "Hi John, nice to see you again. I am okay."

John continued: "Let me introduce you to the other members of our new team. Everyone, please meet Serge. He is with Intel agency."

Everyone answered: "Hi Serge". John, pointing his arm at one of the ladies, kept going: "This is Rebecca Lung. She is a TV reporter with CCB station and a journalist."

I greeted each person with a single move by saying: "Hi everyone, nice to meet you."

Pointing at the other lady, John said: "And this is Juliet Tolleta. Juliet is a TV reporter too. She is with News Today station. And here is Major Rubbens. As you can see Major Rubbens represents the Military and he is an explosives expert."

With a courteous smile Major Rubbens added: "Please call me Hue."

I automatically repeated the "explosives expert" phrase in my head, thinking it is getting more and more interesting. While I was exchanging greetings with new people in the common area, some gentleman, who was sitting at the monitoring station, approached our gathering and offered to show me my bed. I quickly put the things I had with me into the room, noticing that it is not big in size and I do not have a neighbor yet, but the sleeping cradle looks comfortable and returned back to the public hoping to get some leads on our intriguing assignment. No one knew anything. We were just hanging in there for some time, talking about life, watching TV, trying to impress the ladies, until, one by one, two more persons came in. One of them introduced himself as Captain Richard Motrey, a Military expert and the other one was Mr. Mark Donovan. As I understood Mr. Mark Donovan represented some Diplomatic Service or something similar and he was appointed as the commander or the leader of our group. Captain Richard Motrey became my neighbor and Mr. Donovan got another room just for himself. In about an hour's time, the monitoring station man opened the entrance door and requested all of us to follow him. Pretty soon we entered something like a command center, where various people and different equipment could be seen. One gentleman in a very expensive suit moved to the center and addressed the crowd: "Firstly, I would like to thank you all for coming. Secondly, I have to remind you that all of you here have top secret clearance and this upcoming operation requires just that. No one at all is supposed to know what you will be doing for the next while, even your direct supervisors at your official jobs. Thirdly, we have to finish up with some legal issues here and before signing those papers I have to ask all of you — are there any rejections? Does anyone think they would not be able to finish the assignment, which might take much longer than is planned?" The gentleman then looked at each one of us and no one showed any signs of doubt. I realized that the gentleman's name was Mr. X. And it was obvious to me that Mr. X. is a high ranked government official and he was sure that he does not need introduction; everyone knows him or is supposed to know him already. After we signed the papers, Mr. X. asked one of his assistants to provide us with all the details: why we are there and what happened earlier, the present situation and what is expected of us in the near future. The assistant moved slightly aside, so we can see the big screen on the wall, and started his campaign:

"Hi everyone, my name is Marshal Kunnigan. I am with..."
and he named a very serious organization. I thought "each
minute it is getting more and more interesting..." Marshal
continued: "Ladies and Gentlemen, at the beginning of my
speech I would like to inform you that due to the nature of
the business your phones and other electronic equipment
will be monitored closely by our staff. It is not that we do
not trust you, otherwise you would not be here, but we have
to take all the precaution measures to make it safe for you
personally and your families. So, please, do not share a
single word about this operation with anyone. As you all
probably know we use the high tech equipment to gather
Intelligence across the world. And this reliable Intel allows
us to stay on top of the game. I am sure every one of you
heard about our so called ultra-modern drones, which also
go by another name - Unmanned Aerial Vehicle (UAV)."
Then Marshal looked at everyone of us to make sure we
understood his explanation and continued: "A few days ago,
during its mission, one of our state-of-the-Art UAV's was
hijacked by some foreign counter intelligence service and
safely landed at one of the Military bases in that distant
country. And now it is very complicated..."

Suddenly Mr. X. with anger in his voice interrupted the
speaker: "Make it simple."

It became obvious to me that Marshal Kunnigan was
a smart man and he knew his Boss very well, because
right away he was able to make an adjustment: "Yes, one
might say it is illegal to send your flying devices to spy on
other countries, but we see that particular country as a
potential threat and our position is – Better Safe, Than
Sorry. And this is not the first time when the country in
question was able to intercept one of our drones. Casualties

happen. But this particular model, the last captured UAV, has very advanced technological solutions, including stealth technology, so we cannot allow anyone to duplicate or copy the machinery..." Again Marshal took a brief pause probably to check our reactions and catch his breath and moved on with the details: "Now I have to tell you some news Ladies and Gentlemen, some good ones and some not that good. The bad news is – this last incident could easily become a political scandal, which, I am sure; our diplomats will be able to fix. The good news is, the country in question is organizing an exposition to show off their trophies and this will include our drones. They already announced the dates and invited reporters to cover the event. I am not sure how many countries will visit and it does not matter today, since we'll still have all those channels to transmit news. In a matter of hours the whole world will be able to get the information. But for us this upcoming expo is an opportunity to make things right and that is why all of you are here. Do you have any questions so far?"

John raised his hand and said: "My name is John Kalger. The question I want to ask you: Is it known yet how the other guys were able to take control over the drone?"

Marshal automatically looked at Mr. X. like trying to get approval and answered the following: "Today we have a few different versions of the event. For example: if the opposing party were able to send a stronger signal, theoretically, then they probably would have a chance to do just that. We are considering this possibility very carefully. Some time ago the country in question did not have Electronic Warfare of that level. Another version is a malfunction of the device. Our specialists are already looking into all the possibilities and hopefully soon we will have the answers. Any more questions?" No one asked anything and Marshal continued: "As you noticed already there are seven of you who are going into that country to visit the expo. We formed three teams, two persons each and Mr. Donovan will be the head of the operation, staying close to all of you, monitoring the situation and coordinating your actions. According to our plan each team will enter the country of interest from a different territory. Major Rubbens and Captain Motrey, two Military professionals, will form one team. Of course these gentlemen will have different names and legends, the details of which are to follow. The other two teams will consist each of a reporter and a cameraman. Ms. Rebecca and Mr. John will form one team. The other team will be Ms. Juliet and Mr. Serge. Our beautiful ladies, real reporters, do not need any introduction on the world stage, they already covered a lot of stories for their companies from different countries and thus are well known. As for you gentlemen, our new cameramen, your professional training will start tomorrow. Any questions so far?"

John raised his hand again and said: "My name is John Kalger. My question is…"

I did not know what John was doing, but it looked to me like he was trying to get himself noticed by Mr. X. or some other big official by pronouncing his name often. Who knows, what if Mr. X. is looking to hire someone soon?

John continued: "I heard those drones have advanced security features. Is it not possible to remotely eliminate the threat, like to turn on some self-liquidating program or something?"

Marshal, still being patient, started his explanation: "As I told you already, it is not clear yet how the device got into the wrong hands. We are working on it. But what is known exactly, that all the operations carried out by the drone are recorded in the memory of the Unmanned Aerial Vehicle. Yes, the information is coded, but, hypothetically, it does not mean that it could not be decoded. There are a number of International players with appropriate resources, who will be more than happy to join in to help break the code. And moreover, we are afraid that the opposing party might be able to reverse-engineer the chemical components of the UAV's radar-deflecting paint, making a real threat to our stealth technology program and also the aircraft's advanced optics are a big concern too. To summarize everything, we have too much investment into this UAV project that we cannot risk it getting into someone else's possession. Any more questions?"

Everyone was silent, trying to process the information received. Marshal made a sign to a gentleman sitting by the computer and said: "Today I am going to give you all the details of the upcoming operation in a nutshell, so you will be able to understand your role in it. Tomorrow we will start working with each one of you individually and after that in teams."

While Marshal was explaining the purpose of the operation, the man behind the computer made a few moves with the mouse and the video of a drone flying in the air appeared on the big screen. Then it was an aerial view of some area and Marshal made a sign to the computer man to freeze the picture. We could see some kind of a building structure and the surrounding neighborhood on the screen. Marshal commented: "This is the Expo pavilion. There will be two explosions, during the Expo, minutes apart, here and here." Somehow a laser pointer appeared in Marshal's hands and he showed us on the screen where the explosions are supposed to happen. Then he continued: "This will be done to distract security at the event and create panic. Later two independent organizations "Peaceful Citizens" and "Free Riders" will claim the responsibility for the outbursts. Let me assure you, our men here know how to play it safe, so not a single person gets hurt." While saying these last words Marshal stretched his arm towards our Military men and it was clear that he was referring to them when mentioning that no one is supposed to get hurt.

Continuing his explanations, Marshal looked at our beautiful ladies and said: "Two teams with video equipment will be recording the event inside the pavilion. There will also be another commotion at the exhibition area. Mr. Donovan will make sure that the noise is loud. At that time some explosives will be placed onto the drone; at the front and back…" Again Marshal made a sign to the computer man and the blueprint of the pavilion appeared on the screen. "As you can see," continued the speaker, "there are a few exits in the building and the surveillance cameras cover them all, including the space inside the pavilion and the outside territory. But there is always a chance to find some "blind spot" if you know what you are doing and how to do that. For example: one might turn their back towards the security camera and be covered from the front by the body of the exhibition exponent, let's say by a drone or by other people standing nearby and this simple move will allow that individual, using both hands, to attach something to the body of the drone. And it is even easier to do so if you are carrying some photo equipment on your chest. What is important, especially after the drone gets destroyed, is to show your emotions: act according to the situation, be frightened, panic, but still do your job, show professionalism, meaning record everything around you, especially the destroyed drone and create good photo reportage. Also, all of you, particularly the people who will be present on the scene at the time of the event, should be ready to get detained and answer a lot of questions. But there ought not to be any direct proof of your involvement. Preparation is key and we take things seriously. We will make sure that a couple of so called "suspicious" individuals are present at the event to keep the investigators busy..."

Marshal stopped for a moment, glanced at Mr. X. like asking if he wants to add something and not seeing any reaction continued: "This is all for today that we wanted to share with you. The main work starts tomorrow. Do you have any more questions Ladies and Gentlemen?"

No one said anything. Probably each one of us was thinking about the upcoming operation, processing the information received and trying to find weak points in the entire scheme.

A LIPSTICK SITUATION

The next morning, after breakfast, all seven of us went different ways. John Kalger and I were taken to a separate room, where we could see a lot of photo equipment and such. The instructor, a person with countless experience and knowledge of the industry, introduced himself as Ron Knott. He gave each one of us a piece of paper with a number of industry related words written on it. Ron said: "Please, Gentlemen, learn these words and their meaning, it is jargon. Any professional cameraman uses it in their work. For the next while, today and tomorrow to be precise, we will learn how to operate all this gear you can see here and my goal is to teach you to feel comfortable doing it. Do you have any questions so far?"

John, as usual, had a question or two. He said: "Why did you or whoever it was pick me and Serge for this operation?"

The instructor, for a brief moment, thought about whether or not to answer and eventually replied: "The explanation is very simple. We went through a number of different databases checking faces and other physical characteristics of the available agents and eventually made our choice: both you and Serge look almost exactly as the cameramen who work regularly with Rebecca and Juliet. Only minor adjustments are needed. But these gentlemen, real professionals, they do not have the security clearance you have and they do not know about our maneuver and that our beautiful ladies are Intelligence agents as well. Journalists and reporters need official approval to work in some countries and places. And both teams, Rebecca and her assistant and Juliet and her assistant have already received permission to cover the event. So, the idea is to eject their official partners for some period of time, until everything is finished, and you gentlemen will step in, using the names and documents of those men. By the way, you will start learning your new legends tomorrow. Any more questions?"

Both John and I were silent, thinking about the complicity and yet the simplicity of the idea. Ron, seeing our thoughtfulness, continued: "This video and voice recording equipment is for you John and the other set is for Serge. They are almost identical – both Rebecca's and Juliet's teams use them. You, each, will have two sets on you: a photo camera with spare telephoto zoom lenses and a professional video and voice recording camera they use to produce movies and news on TV. I know it is going to be difficult to carry one camera on your shoulder or in your hand and at the same time carry the other one on your chest, plus hold on to the spare telephoto zoom lenses, but you will get used to it. You need to do it and here is why," then Ron took one of the telephoto zoom lenses belonging to one of the cameras and said: "See this lens, do you notice anything unusual about it?"

John quickly, like it was some kind of a competition, replied: "Looks expensive though, similar to a journalist's apparatus they show on TV, especially when you watch sports..."

The instructor explained: "Yes, it is pricey, but that particular piece was modified by our technicians. For an average eye it looks exactly as you said John, but see this front part here, it was added to the device on purpose. This nosepiece has some high tech explosives in it, very powerful and yet almost undetectable stuff. With the help of a little button, right here, you can take apart these two pieces roughly in no time. And after you have separated it, the timer starts. This cap will detonate in thirty seconds. The main idea is to attach that hotheaded element to the captured drone and the explosives are made in such a way that after the blow, which is not strong, just enough to break the cover, the inside material will spread around the area melting and burning everything in its way, destroying the drone and all its equipment... For people who happen to be around the device at the time of the explosion, two meters distance from the drone will be enough to stay safe."

After the instructor took the pieces apart, explaining to us how it works, I automatically looked at a wristwatch and at the exit door, ready to run out. Noticing my fears Ron added: "Do not worry Serge, right now it is safe; no batteries inside, we have to practice first." Then he placed one of the cameras with the big telephoto zoom lenses on his chest, took the other one, the professional video camera, into his right arm and said: "When you have this camera in your hand like that and you need to lift it up on your shoulder to start shooting the news, to do just that you have to help with your other hand. You move your free arm like this, quickly, while continuing the same move you push this button on the lens, right here, and turn the secretly added cap counterclockwise; see right here - it gets separated from the main body - and you still continue the same move, acting like your reaching for the camera. Attach this piece to the body of the drone, it will stick to it like glue, and again continue the move and take the video camera right here and lift it up on your shoulder. It is a difficult move, but with some practice, like a thousand times today, you will be able to do it. You will be covered from the front by your partner or by the drone. The view from behind will show only that you have just lifted your equipment up, preparing it for work."

Both John and I were looking at the instructor in disbelieve, questioning everything that was said and done. But Ron, with a single move, was able to dismiss all of our doubts. Probably he practiced that move himself a couple of zillion times before, showing off his skills to us or maybe he was just really talented. Anyway, we started practicing all those fancy moves and let me tell you; in a couple of hours I thought that the job of a cameraman is a tough one. Sometime later we had a break and after the break we continued with the exercise, learning moves, getting used to carrying the equipment and feeling miserable. In the evening, when we returned back to the common area, we had to go through the jargon lists that Ron gave us. First we memorized the words and their meanings and then tested each other's knowledge by asking questions. The rest of the people from our team had their own things to do and everyone was busy.

The next morning, and until lunch time, we kept practicing the moves that the instructor showed us and we made it even more difficult; this time Ron himself tested our knowledge of the industry related words from the jargon list. He would say something and we had to translate his words into everyday language of average people. It was almost fun, except we still could not move properly and fast enough and sometimes we confused the jargon words with their meanings. After lunch, we all, including Rebecca and Juliet, but excluding all the other members of our group, moved to a different facility where we were surprised to discover a replica of the secret drone. Seeing our excitement Ron, the instructor, said: "There are a few reasons why this UAV is here. And one of them is to teach you how to accurately identify when shown at the exhibition, if the drone is the authentic one and not a fake copy. Another reason is to give you an opportunity to practice your moves in similar conditions to the upcoming operation. This place has three so called security cameras: there, there and there. Also, keep in mind that some hidden equipment might be positioned somewhere in the area too. So, you first have to make sure that nothing is concealed around the drone's spot, which could potentially lead to a failure, because sometimes cameras are hidden in people's dresses and purses. Then you need to find a proper point for yourselves from which you will be able to safely and clandestinely place the lens's cap onto the drone."

Rebecca and Juliet have not looked surprised or puzzled when Ron mentioned that we have to place something somewhere. Probably the ladies already knew about the whole diagram of the forthcoming operation. In the meanwhile the instructor continued:

"Now let me explain and show you how to positively identify if the UAV is authentic or not." Then Ron shifted closer to the drone and pulled some lipstick from his pocket saying: "See this lipstick?"

The ladies, Rebecca and Juliet, instantly looked at each other with a smile of understanding and almost simultaneously rolled their eyes like sending a message: "Look who is finally out of the closet". Both John and I were just standing there, not showing any emotions, smiling politely and listening to the instructor.

For the meantime Ron continued: "It is not your regular lipstick that you can buy at any store. This one was made exclusively for you guys, for this operation, and it has some specific chemical components in it. This lipstick is like litmus paper. First, one of the ladies should put some of this lipstick, just a little bit, on a piece of paper and this must be done before going into the pavilion, not to attract attention, and then she has to slide that piece of paper against the body of the drone, like this. If the drone is the real thing, then the color of this lipstick should change, becoming black. If it stays the same red, then you know the drone is not authentic, it is a fake copy. And if it is a replica, then you just do your coverage of the event, not destroying anything and leave. And if security guys somehow notice that you are scratching the drone and ask you what you are doing, you can always say that you were removing some dirt, making the drone look shiny and attractive… By the way both of you ladies should have this paper with lipstick in your possession before going inside the pavilion. And you have to decide between yourselves, according to the situation at the expo, which one of you has to check the "bona fide" of the UAV."

Rebecca said: "May I ask you a question Ron?"

The instructor replied: "Sure."

Rebecca continued: "Why don't we decide right now who does what?"

Ron answered: "We do not know what is going to happen at the event. You are journalists and quite well known to certain people. Someone might decide to talk to you at the expo or something. I suggest you guys see who is closer to the drone; whoever has the better opportunity to do the job, they should do it. I want you, after you have the result, to give a sign to all the rest. Just raise your thumb up, like greeting people or showing that everything is good."

Rebecca said: "Makes sense. Thank you Ron. So, thumbs up if the thing is real and if it is not, then the opposite."

Everyone laughed. Ron continued with his instructions: "Right now I am going to sit in the next room and stare at the monitors. I am going to be watching your actions, starting from the beginning. You are two teams, making your own reportages about the event. You have to find your positions and you have to place the lenses' caps onto the drone, preferably one at the front and the other one at the back of the UAV. Then we will analyze what went right and what went wrong. Is everything clear?"

We all answered: "Yes."

"Then lets proceed," said Ron and disappeared from our view.

We practiced the specified routine for about two hours, changing positions, trying to find better ways to do the job. Periodically the instructor would invite us to the tech room to look at the recordings of our actions and to show and explains to us the mistakes that were made.

Eventually, when we realized what is expected from us and became pretty skilled doing it, the instructor came out of his shelter and said: "Now, Ladies and Gentlemen, you are ready for the next level task. Let me explain. First, I wanted to make sure that you feel confident doing all those fancy moves and stuff and that is why we began our training with simple things. Now I would like to provide you with some additional information. As you understand, the security at the event will be tight. Almost certainly no radio and electronic equipment will be allowed inside the pavilion. What is also possible, that some kind of a perimeter will be installed around the exponent, so, no one could touch it. Also, there is a possibility that motion sensors will be placed around the drone and in addition to it a security alarm, similar, for example, to a car alarm, might be installed on the drone itself. Another scenario involves the placement of the UAV inside a glass cubicle. Again this might be done to prevent anyone from any contact with the device. And if this is the case, obviously you people would not be able to do your job. In this situation our commandos will demolish the thing during the night time. Of course it will be obvious in whose interests the gadget was destroyed, but again it is hard to prove it. And as usual, some local organization will step forward proudly claiming the responsibility for the happening. Yes, it will cost us some money, but the possibility of someone copying the technology and then using it for wrong purposes or selling it to others, is far more dangerous."

We stood, all of us, in front of the instructor, listening to every word he said. At this point in time it was totally clear that the task at hand is not as simple as it might have looked initially. We have to make a lot of important decisions ourselves, based on the situation at the expo. The good thing was that we had skilled and smart people and we knew what to expect.

In the meanwhile Ron continued: "As you probably understood already, we are not going to waste our time with you on the third "glass cubicle" scenario. Some other people are working on it already. We need to focus on the second possibility. Let's name it "A lipstick situation". Everything stays the same; you still have to check if the exponent is the real UAV, you still have to find good "blind" spots and you still have to be able to quickly place the caps on the drone. What is going to be new here is that we are bringing in two more persons for our practice. Remember Marshal Kunnigan mentioned that a couple of "suspicious" individuals will be present at the event. These will be two criminals known to local Police. Also, Ladies and Gentlemen, keep in mind the thirty second gap before the devices explode and you have to get to a safe distance during this time, which is, as I mentioned earlier, two meters. And let me assure you it is very possible to do just that, considering the fact that professional sprinters run the one hundred meters distance under ten seconds. It also means that the explosion devices need to be placed on the drone right away, one after another or at the same time."

John interrupted the instructor saying: "So, basically we have ten seconds opening for two teams, no sorry, for three teams, including the bad guys, to do the job?"

Ron answered: "You got it right John. When both teams are around the drone area making their reportages, one of the criminal guys will try to steal a wallet from one of the cameramen, because the cameraman has his hands occupied holding a camera. Then this individual will try to fly away and the cameraman is to catch the guy right around the drone. And as you figured out already this will be the opportunity to place the explosives onto the UAV. When the "stealing" happens, the partner of that cameraman, one of you our beautiful ladies, will start yelling "Thief, thief…" to distract the public. At the same time the second criminal will try to steal a wallet from the other cameraman and it is going to be exactly the same scenario. The thief gets caught close to the drone; the reporter lady will scream "Help" and the explosives are ready to burst."

I looked at John and the ladies; each person was silent and had a serious face. Everyone understood that one thing is to explain something in simple words, in safe conditions, but the other thing is to really perform the task when required. There is always something unexpected that happens and also, no one yet cancelled the so called "human factor" rule. But again, we have a good and skilled workforce, amazing instructors and what was also important – we spent sufficient time preparing for the event and preparation is key. When you are prepared and are able to anticipate something, the success will come.

Ron, in the meantime, called in two more men to play bad guys and we also installed the two meters perimeter around the UAV. The new level of practice has begun. First, one of the ladies, Rebecca to be exact, accidentally dropped her microphone on the floor. The microphone somehow ended its movement under the drone. Not saying a word Rebecca quickly entered the secured perimeter and like trying to hold her balance picked up the microphone at the same time sliding the lipstick paper against the body of the drone. Then she quickly got back behind the perimeter saying: "I am okay, no worries" and raised the big thumbs up.

We practiced hard again. This time it was different. John and I had to run after the "bad" guys, breaking the secured perimeter and trying to catch those "thieves" as close as possible to the drone. At the same time, we had to place the caps with the explosives on the UAV. John suggested that he will place the explosives at the front of the drone leaving the rear part for me. I agreed with him quickly because it was reasonable in this situation and to know who does what and when it should be done is a part of the job too. And we are a team.

The instructor kept inviting us periodically to the tech room, to look at the recordings of our actions and to show and explains to us the mistakes that were made. Eventually, Ron was satisfied with our work. Later in the evening, when we were tired, hungry and exhausted, he called it a day. But before we left, Ron showed us some pictures of the "bad" guys whom we may possibly see at the expo. We needed to remember their faces in order to not run after someone else accidentally. Also, the instructor gave another assignment specifically to John and me. During the rest of the day and including a few hours of the next morning we had to go through the files of the real cameramen, memorizing their legends, learning about their families and habits, looking at the pictures.

This last night at the facility I slept like a baby, but still saw a lot of drones, video equipment and scary explosions in my dreams. I would not call these visions a nightmare, but it was very close to it.

The next morning, before we left for the airport, Marshal Kunnigan repeated his instructions to all of us, to all members of the team. He reminded about the importance of the upcoming operation and the possible danger alongside it. In addition to it, Marshal reiterated the whole scheme of our maneuver, which, if you look at it briefly, sounded like this: two separate explosions outside the expo pavilion, then some commotion inside the exhibition area, then so called "thieves" get into action, one by one, then, then, then... And eventually the drone get's destroyed.

Mr. X. too, took his part in the last moments' tutoring

saying: "All of you here are brave and professional people. You serve your country with enormous courage and honor. I do not have any doubt that the aim of the upcoming operation will be achieved. And I, myself, am proud to be a part of this team, personally selecting some of you for this big task at hand. Today I do not want to talk about the danger of this action and I do not want to talk about the reward that awaits you after you accomplish what was planned. I just want to wish you good luck, and help us God."

MAKING IT SIMPLE

After all of the instructions and the hard practice of the last two days, each team went to the airport at different times and probably using diverse routes. This was done for security reasons and not to attract unnecessary attention. I thought that move was reasonable; what if, hypothetically speaking, someone knew about the business we had to carry out? Then the use of just one grenade or of something similar would be enough to take care of everyone. It proved my supposition that Intelligence professionals do not take those types of chances by keeping all the key people together in one car or in a van.

When Juliet and I were checking in for the scheduled flight, somehow I had that picture in my head: an angry Mr. X. saying to his assistant "Make it simple". I thought this is a very smart strategy to keep things uncomplicated. And it is good that we have a great team of high level experts supporting our group; the experts, who did their best to train us properly and who reminded us a colossal number of times about the importance of this rule. Very often, people in general, tend to over think something or worry too much. And that is exactly what had happened to me. All that time during our travel, going through a number of security checks at airports in different countries, and until we got to the last point of our travel, I thought I was carrying the real explosion lens with me, with all my video and photo equipment. Of course I did not worry much leaving our city; I knew I had all the possible support there. The scariest moment of the journey was upon our arrival to the final destination: the "expodrone" host country. When we landed at the local airport, Juliet was the first in line at the passport control point and I was the next person to go after her. The border official briefly looked at my partner, who was charming and smiling politely, then checked something in her passport and with a heavy accent said:

"What is the reason for your visit?"

Still looking happy, Juliet explained that we are visiting on business and that she is a TV reporter. The official returned Juliet's passport and let her go. Now it was my turn. I put a very friendly expression on my face and handed "my" passport to the man. The official looked at me watchfully, then compared the image in front of him with the photo in the passport, at the same time looking at the height scale, and at that very exact moment his phone rang. I was all tense inside, but still had a pleasant facial expression, thinking what could be wrong? It turned out the phone call was about some other matter, because the official said something back to someone on the other end of the line and returned the passport to me. I was free to go. We did not have any problems with customs officers; they just suspiciously looked at our luggage, which was not that large at all, but said nothing and let us go.

Going to the hotel, where a couple of rooms were booked for us already, we took a taxi from the airport. The cab driver was not all that talkative and we were happy with that. Later in the evening, when I was sitting in my room preparing for the big day, someone knocked on the entrance door. I thought it is room service or something, but to my surprise it was Mr. Donovan himself. He had some bag in his hands. I recognized the bag because I had the same one in my possession with a "loaded" photo camera inside it. It turned out I was mistaken because Mr. Donovan quickly stepped in, just a little bit, to get out of the view of the passageway camera and at the same time not getting into the room and said:

"Hi, my name is Mr. Donovan. I am looking for Mr. MacKenzie. The reception clerk sent me here."

While he was saying these words he made a sign to me to exchange the bags with him. Also, he made a sign that the room might be under surveillance. Luckily the bag I had with the same type of photo camera was sitting on the floor, right by the entrance door, so that I did not have to do anything; I just slightly moved the bag with my leg for Mr. Donovan to reach it. Mr. Donovan rapidly exchanged the bags showing no emotions at all.

After the exchange was done I answered:

"I am sorry Sir, you have the wrong room number, we do not have anyone under that name here."

Mr. Donovan replied: "Oh, I am so sorry," and then he left.

Now I knew that he gave me the "real thing", which he probably had delivered here through some diplomatic channels.

In the morning, and after we had breakfast, Juliet and I went to the expo. We were prepared: we had all the possible papers, documents and of course we had our video and photo equipment with us. Juliet looked great and seemed to be calm, but I knew somewhere inside she was almost on the edge. That is the difference between professional people and amateurs. Professionals can pull themselves together, they are able to control their nerves and actions and perform under almost any circumstances. Amateurs, on the other hand, do not have the same training and very often cannot manage themselves well enough to execute the task at hand. And my partner for this mission was a real professional. She handled herself very well. I was nervous a little bit too, but the trick for success is to be able to relax and save some energy for the big moment when you need it.

When we were entering the exhibition area, it was obvious to us that the place is under very strict security. You could see people in uniform here, there and everywhere. Serious faces, observant glances, you could even sense some tension in the air. If an artist was to draw a work of art of the exhibition place and its surroundings, they would probably name the painting "A peaceful war zone". That was the first impression we got after arriving to the place.

It took us another ten – fifteen minutes to go through all the possible security checks before we entered the expo pavilion. I got the feeling that the people in charge of the occasion thought of all the possible measures to eliminate any threat to the event. The security guards carefully checked all our papers, we had to go through some electronic frames, similar to the ones they use at airports and the guards also vigilantly checked our video and photo equipment. I put an "I am angry, but I understand it's your job" mask on my face and patiently waited for the green light from the officials to get into the territory. Juliet did not show any emotions. She was just following the instructions from the guards and it seemed to me that it worked perfectly. I even thought "always obey those in power and you will be fine".

When we eventually passed the cordon and entered the

exhibition area, John Kalger and Rebecca Lung were already in there. Both our groups professionally greeted each other, showing respect and at the same time keeping some distance between the teams. We knew that the organizers will be watching every single person in the area, and we did not want to attract unnecessary attention. It was time for us to do our job, and both teams, using different routes, slowly moved to the specified area, where the secret drone was placed on some kind of a stand for observation. The place looked almost exactly as we expected it to be with some more various UAVs around. While moving forward and discussing with Juliet the best position for the news reportage I was surreptitiously scanning the area, looking for the security cameras, determining the possible blind spots, and at the same time trying to locate the familiar faces of the so called "bad guys". If I did not know what I was looking for, then I would probably not be able to identify these gentlemen ever. It took me almost a couple of minutes to realize that the man in a nice suit, standing not far away from Juliet and looking at the exponents, is the chap I was looking for. The other one, dressed the same well, was near John and Rebecca. There were many other people in the area, including Mr. Donovan. I noticed him too. Mr. Donovan was in a group of some sort of officials and these people looked so important, that every other visitor was quickly moving away, giving way for the group to pass. The exponents at the exhibition did not have the secured perimeter around them, but there was a soldier proudly standing at the side of each drone. The good news was that the combatants were standing at the front of each UAV and if you moved behind their back, they would not be able to see what you are doing. But the bad news was that the soldiers standing on the other side of the passageway were facing their comrades, covering the missing areas.

While I was assessing the situation, Rebecca and John were already around the drone, ready to proceed. Acting innocent and being calm, Rebecca, like it happened at practice before, "accidentally" dropped her microphone on the floor and quickly picked it up "unintentionally" touching the drone. On John's question: "Are you okay?"

She raised her thumbs up saying: "I am fine, thank you, just dropped the thing," and with a happy facial expression she waved her microphone in the air. Rebecca's behavior was above suspicion for any untrained eye, but for us, her teammates, we knew what was actually going on and that the drone was authentic, the right one.

Mr. Donovan probably saw the sign given to us by Rebecca, because a few moments later we heard a very loud explosion somewhere outside the pavilion area. At first no one understood anything; people were just standing and looking at each other in surprise. Then someone in uniform quickly ran out of the building to find out what had happened and a moment later we heard the second explosion on the other side of the exposition structure. The real panic started inside the exhibition area and outside of it. One of the ladies from Mr. Donovan's group of important people fell down on the floor, not showing any vital signs at all and another woman yelled "Help, help". Some of the screaming visitors started running back and forth around the area without any understanding of the situation and kept asking the same "what happened" questions. At that very moment Rebecca Lung roared "Thief, thief…" and I saw John Kalger and the soldier, who was on his duty protecting the drone, trying to apprehend one of the "bad" guys, who was showing some signs of resistance. At that very moment I knew it was the time for me to act too. Fortunately, or maybe because of the hard practice we had, the other "bad" man did his move on me too and I ran after him with all my photo and video equipment, while Juliet screamed "Help someone. Please." The "bad" guy was smart; he stopped at the rear end of the drone and shamelessly pretended that he is looking at the exponent, like he was really interested in the advanced technological solutions used on the device. I did not hesitate a bit and quickly disconnected the "loaded" cap from the photo lens and placed it on the drone with my left arm. After that, with the same left arm, which was free now, I caught the "bad" man by the sleeve of his expensive jacket. The video camera in my right hand was getting in the way all the time, but I was able to move it slightly behind my back.

The man, like a good actor, showed real signs of surprise on his face for my actions and said something angry to me in a foreign language. I did not understand a thing, but I knew we had to move aside from the UAV, which was about to explode in a very brief moment. I was sure we all kept in mind the safe two meters distance from the drone, to which we had to move, and the time frame needed for the devices to detonate. Playing my role and looking at the man I realized that no damage is done, the wallet I had with me is in my pocket, where it was supposed to be, and I let the man go. Still screaming something furiously at me the man disappeared somewhere. I did not even try to see where he went; no time for that, I had a job to do. Like at practice, I intentionally turned my back to the drone, lifted the camera up and started videotaping everything, all the chaos and commotion around me. My skilled journalist partner reacted right away and I focused the camera on her. I even thought the more dangerous the situation is - the more excited people of that profession become. In the meanwhile, holding her microphone, Juliet was saying: "Good day everyone. I am Juliet Tolleta..."

At that very moment the first device at the front part of the drone had exploded and initially no one understood what had just happened. The sound of the explosion was not loud at all, and some smoke and the smell of something melting and burning started spreading around everywhere. I shifted the camera from Juliet focusing it on the drone, and the second device, at the rear part of the UAV, had just detonated with the same sound and smoke as the first one. As it often happens in situations like that, the majority of people around the area were under confusion initially, then the confusion transformed into panic and, eventually terrified, they started running out of the building. Some of the soldiers reacted very quickly and brought fire extinguishers to stop the drone from burning. It did not help though. The UAV was destroyed and I had the evidence of it. Eventually, the security guards and soldiers took the situation under control. They speedily built a perimeter around the building and asked everyone to go out of the pavilion, but stay inside the perimeter until further notice.

During all these events, for some period of time, I totally forgot about Mr. Donovan, Rebecca Lung and John Kalger. When I saw them, Mr. Donovan was with his group of important people, watching a couple of medical professionals working on the distressed lady, who was still laying on the floor. Rebecca and John were nearby, arguing about something with the security guards and soldiers. One of the guards approached Juliet and me and gesticulated to stop videotaping and that we should go out of the expo pavilion. We decided not to argue and followed the directions.

When we went out of the building, we saw the following picture: the security guards and officials created a few checking points in the area and people were hurriedly lining up there in order to get away from this disastrous place. Also, there were a number of fire department trucks on both sides of the expo structure, as well as police cars and ambulances.

As soon as it was our turn to go through the security check, the person in charge asked us to surrender our video and photo equipment, but promised to return it later when they finished with the examination of the recordings. In addition to that, the security people wrote down all our information, where we are staying and everything, and they asked us not to leave the country while the investigation is going on or until further notice.

Later in the evening, sitting in my room at the hotel and analyzing the past events of the day, I heard someone knock on my door. It was Juliet. She asked me to go with her into her room; she said we have a visitor, a diplomat from some diplomatic mission, who wants to talk to us.

The visitor was a gentleman unknown to me, around forty five – fifty years old, dressed in business attire and with a "no kidding around" facial expression. He introduced himself as Mr. Aghar Khalmani. After the exchange of initial pleasantries Mr. Khalmani said: "Miss Rebecca Lung, a citizen of our country and a journalist, was detained today together with her cameraman at the expo event in this city. Right away Miss Rebecca Lung asked local establishment to contact us, but there was a delay for unknown reasons and just a couple of hours ago we finally received several updates on the situation. It does not look good. The authorities accuse Miss Rebecca and her partner of spying for some foreign Intelligence Service and threaten them with imprisonment."

Both Juliet and I simultaneously looked at each other; we totally understood the risk involved and the possible consequences of our actions for us and for our colleagues and friends, who were detained by the Counter Intelligence Service of this country and probably, at this exact point in time, were in the process of answering tough questions. When we were leaving the exhibition area we saw Rebecca and John arguing about something with the security guards and soldiers, but we did not want to compromise our mission and acted according to the protocol.

After a brief pause Juliet said: "Sir, do you know the exact reason why they were placed in custody; the allegation of spying sounds fishy and the word espionage has quite a broad definition?"

The diplomat answered: "So far I told you everything I know and as soon as we are finished here I will go straight to the detention center to visit Miss Rebecca and her partner."

At that very moment a telephone rang somewhere. It turned out it was the phone belonging to our guest. Mr. Khalmani answered it, not saying much, listened to someone on the other end of the line and then said: "As I suspected, both of you are under surveillance. That is why I am here to warn you. We do not know the plans of the locals regarding your stay here and we do not know what way they might go to put some pressure on you to force you to make mistakes. They might not touch you at all or they might go through the official way by blaming you of something too, or they might use some criminal elements to get what they want. In any case, my people will be nearby watching the development of the situation and the two of you."

I decided to ask Mr. Khalmani a question, which bothered me for the past few minutes and said: "There was very tight security at the expo event. I noticed a lot of officials, soldiers, cameras and so on. Do you know Sir, how advanced these people are on technology?"

"Good question," answered the man and continued: "It is our job, yours and mine, to know who does what and who has what. And as I understood your query correctly, by technology you mean if this country has the same advanced technical solutions that we have. For example: the programs we use at our airports that detect unusual behavior or terror threats and could pick up a single dangerous person out of a thousand of normal passengers or a face recognition software as another example and so on. And my answer will be - I do not know. I am sure you see my point – your assignment was to cover the event which should not have happened initially."

I thought the diplomat is right, and I totally understood him. This world is changing very rapidly and if yesterday someone did not have something, it does not mean they will not have that thing tomorrow. And even if today you have the best Intelligence in the world, which obviously gives you certain advantages, this does not mean that you are always ahead of the competition.

In the meanwhile Mr. Khalmani looked at his watch and said: "As I was informed both of you were asked not to leave the country without permission. And your departure tickets are booked for the day after tomorrow. So, the time

is pressing. What I want you to do during these two days;
I want you to stay in your hotel and do not go anywhere.
Just watch TV, relax and act average. In the near future
my colleagues and I, through our channels, will place some
pressure on local authorities to force them to return your
equipment and to let all of you go and leave the country."

Juliet replied: "We do not worry about ourselves Sir;
we worry about our friends and colleagues. Please Mr.
Khalmani, do everything possible to help them and if you
need our assistance, you know where to find us."

Mr. Aghar Khalmani answered: "Your emotional
response is not a surprise for me and I did not expect
anything less. You are noble people and you do a great job
serving your country. All I can do is to assure you that we are
going to do the whole lot in our power to free your friends.
And we are going to do it as fast as we can. Let's hope for the
best, good luck and help us God." And the ambassador left
Juliet's room, hopefully going right away to the detention
center, as he promised, to help our colleagues.

The next day my partner and I spent at the hotel, sitting
in our rooms, worrying about John and Rebecca, and briefly
meeting each other for snacks. Nothing interesting happened
at all during this time, with the exception that later in the
evening Mr. Donovan showed up at Juliet's room for a split
second and informed us about the present circumstances.

After the exchange of greetings Mr. Donovan said:
"I have some good news. According to our sources the
authorities of this town do not have any clear evidence of the
involvement of our citizens into the last outrageous event.
Moreover, a couple of suspiciously oriented organizations
took the responsibility for all that chaos, which happened
yesterday, and for the extreme explosions at the expo. The

news went global. Many TV and radio stations around the world, as well as numerous newspapers, spread the news blaming the local regime of terrorizing its own people and of torturing foreign visitors, who, by the way, were legally invited here to visit this exhibition. So far we did not receive any response yet from the local establishment, but the International Scandal is in the air and the pressure on these people in power, the decision makers, is rising. We are not taking any chances and will keep doing our best to free the innocent."

While Mr. Donovan delivered his dominant speech, speaking like a politician, I realized that his words were probably aimed at someone else, who was not in this room, but who was possibly listening to our conversation. Politics, it is like a game. It is not about who is right and who is wrong; it is about outplaying your opponents.

After the quick update on the state of affairs, the ambassador left the hotel, wishing us good luck and encouraging us to stay positive and strong. We automatically wished him the same in return, because we all needed good luck. And sometimes to be lucky requires a lot of hard work and preparation, anticipation and research, desire to succeed and positive thinking. You have to be lucky to be lucky!

But before Mr. Donovan left, he gave us his last instructions. He said: "If you need to go anywhere, most likely to the police department to pick up your stuff and to the airport for your departure tomorrow, please call the emergency number you have and someone from the Embassy will send a car for you. You will recognize the car by its license plate. That's the least we can do today to eliminate any risk of worsening the situation."

The next morning, still laying in bed, I heard the

telephone ring in my room. It was Juliet. She said she just got a call from the people in charge of the investigation and they said we are free to leave the country today and can pick up our stuff anytime we want, even right now. It was still early in the morning, so we decided to vacate the hotel at midday, then go to the address given to us by the authorities to pick up our photo and video equipment and after that we decided to go directly to the airport. It's always better to play it safe and we were not in the mood for shopping or sightseeing anyway. Thoughts about John and Rebecca, who still were in custody, shaded our minds.

Stay Positive

When we arrived at the specified location, the officer in charge carefully looked at our papers, like trying to find some reason not to return the gear, which belonged to us. We patiently waited for the man to do his job, not showing any emotions. Eventually the bureaucrat realized that everything is in order. What is more, just before we left, the man had found the strength to apologize for all the inconvenience we had. I got the feeling that the man was honest and sincere in expressing his sympathy.

At the airport, it was still too early for our flight; we decided to kill the time by sitting at some cafeteria, talking about life and drinking coffee. In situations like this you keep all your true thoughts to yourself. Any Counter Intelligence people would be more than happy to get as much as possible out of you when you feel secure and that the danger is gone. And there are a number of ways to do just that. Juliet too, knew the rules and she played accordingly.

I was still worried a little bit about the legitimacy of my papers at the passport control point and would continue to be so until we were in the air, but with some proper training you learn to deal with your emotions and do not show any signs of being creepy.

My partner and I had to change a couple of flights before we finally landed in our city's airport. All this travel could be slightly difficult, but if you look at it as an opportunity to see the world, even from the airplane's window, and to learn something new about different cultures, at the same time trying to relax, sleep or watch movies, and read something useful and interesting while on board of the aircraft, you will be fine.

At the airport, after we completed all the necessary procedures like average travelers and exited to the arrival area, someone from the News Today station, where Juliet works, suddenly appeared out of the crowd of impatient people and called her name. The man was sent there by his corporation to meet us. When we got into the company's vehicle, I knew that one or two more automobiles from some other very well known to me organization will be around that car all the time, watching our backs, to make sure that we are safe and were not followed. All of this was just precautionary measures because meticulous individuals belonging to the Intelligence Service of that country, from which we arrived a minute ago, might be in the area too, doing their job. You have to respect your opposition and not take any chances, especially when your friends and coworkers are still in the hands of these people, who are obviously upset after losing the high tech UAV, the drone, which could potentially move their fatherland way ahead in developing technologically advanced machinery.

Following the initial exchange of "How are you?" and similar, the driver, without asking anything else, took us directly to the same building, from which we left to the airport a few days ago. Probably the man was a good psychologist; he just looked at our faces and understood that we are not in the mood to talk. Again, the security guards asked both Juliet and I to proceed to the already familiar section "C". We were placed in some kind of a quarantine or isolation, where we had to write detailed reports about our tricky mission and all that related stuff. We did not argue; it is standard procedure if you are involved in that line of work.

After we were done with the reports, we still had some time to chill out, while our colleagues did their best to check the situation and the surroundings to make sure it is safe for us to leave the facility and go back to our regular duties. Finally, once we got the clearance, I surrendered all the equipment, all the papers and documents I had to the folks in charge, picked up my things, said "good bye" to everyone and left. Using this opportunity I could have easily asked my superiors for a day or two of vacation time, but I knew I had a lot of work to do, including my official and nonofficial assignments.

The very next morning, as a good employee, I showed up at our office at the regular time, looking fresh and sharp, smart and sober, ready to move mountains. With years of experience and with the desire to succeed you learn to be professional.

I was sitting at my desk, going through the papers, trying to set priorities of what to do first and what to do next, when Kristina passed by. She knew that after some absence from the office I needed a little time for myself, to bring my thoughts and work in order. Looking directly at me Kristina just said: "Welcome back", then she touched her wristwatch and added: "See you at lunch time". I quickly answered: "Thank you", and "Okay".

Keeping in mind my upcoming appointment with The Goblin, to whom I tried to report the first thing in the morning, but was told to come back later, I was still thinking about John and Rebecca. How are they? The thought that these angry Counter Intelligence people in that distant country could easily torture them physically and mentally or not give them any food at all, was placing me in a state of craziness. I knew I could not help John and Rebecca in this situation, but my prayer might and I was praying for them every free single moment I had. And also I thought about Romeo. How is he? Obviously this young gentleman needs help. If Kristina wishes to talk to me about Romeo, this could mean that something had happened or she has new information, some news to share. My thoughts were interrupted by a ringing of the phone. It was director Goldberg. The Goblin wanted to see me.

When I entered his study, the director looked thoughtful and considerate. He said: "I know the circumstances of your travel Serge. Do not worry; our people are doing everything in their power to free your friends. We have a lot of leverage and I am sure in the near future this issue will be resolved."

I was not surprised at all that The Goblin knew everything or almost everything about our voyage adventures, but the director himself decided to clarify the situation and said: "Mr. X. called me. He claims you and your colleagues did a great job out there. Congratulations!"

I just answered: "Sir, if you or someone else you know is able to help our captured friends and associates, please do so. John and Rebecca deserve the best, they risk their lives serving this country and we need to do our part to save them."

Director Goldberg once again assured me that this game has moved to another level and very influential people are involved now. These good citizens, the folks in power, they do their best to prove the innocence of our men and women and are looking at all the possibilities and opportunities to do just so. Also, the director asked me if I need any help with my regular job duties. I answered that today morning, before speaking to him, I had a chance to go through all the files I have in my possession and expressed confidence that I am okay. If you are an organized man and plan your work, this helps a lot. And I consider myself to be a well thought-out and reliable employee. For example, if I finished everything I planned for today, I do not just sit there, at my desk, doing nothing. I try to anticipate what is coming in the near future and do tomorrow's tasks and if I finished them all as well, I do the job for the next day. This little trick helps to save a lot of time and nerves. In our line of duty all the workforce members periodically get tossed around to help someone or somewhere else. In addition to the mentioned above I was not sure if The Goblin needed any information from me regarding Romeo, because during these past few days Kristina was at the office and she probably updated him on present affairs concerning this young man, but I still mentioned that we are meeting with Kristina at lunch time to bring me up to date on the subject.

When we finished our conversation, director Goldberg wished the best of luck to all of us, including those not present in the room at the moment and recommended that I stay positive, good things might happen. I, in my turn, asked the director to keep me on a loop regarding John and Rebecca, if he happened to know anything about them, and offered to help if my assistance was needed.

As was planned beforehand we met with Kristina at lunch time to discuss how we can help Romeo. I suggested to talk about the matter in my car. We decided to circle a little bit somewhere in the area close to our office and have a discussion. While being absent, I missed driving around in my Mercedes and as soon as I had the opportunity to do just that, I jumped into the motor vehicle right away. Of course the auto was a little bit dusty inside and outside, but thirty minutes of my precious time changed the situation and the appearance of that piece of finest machinery. Now the automobile looked nice and shiny.

Kristina did not ask me anything about my last assignment; being a real professional she knew how to act in situations like that. She went straight to the business by saying:

"Romeo is out of the hospital. It's been two days already. Actually he is out of the hospital for the second time in a row. I had a chance to talk to him."

Seeing a look of confusion on my face she added: "Do not worry, physically he is okay; otherwise they would not let him go. What I am worrying about is his mental state. When he was out of the hospital the first time, the very same night he called the Police saying that there is a dead body in a car at some parking lot. When the Police arrived, they did not find anything in that car and took Romeo back to the hospital. This time the hospital workers placed him into the department which deals with psychological problems. I thought they are going to keep Romeo in there for a while, to do some assessment of his emotional state and to find the paramount ways to help him. What is difficult to understand is that instead of a proper treatment, they, the medical professionals, let him go the very next morning. The doctor explained that the hospital cannot keep patients in if they, the patients, do not want to stay. I know this sounds puzzling, but these are the rules."

The information my partner told me was interesting and beyond my understanding: is it proper procedure to let a mentally unstable person decide what is best for them? I could not answer that question and just exclaimed: "How did you find out about all of that?" Then added: "Is there any chance for us to lend a hand to that young gentleman?"

Kristina replied: "In response to your first question I have to say: you know how it usually happens in life, this was a chain reaction. The Police informed Romeo's family, the father talked to director Goldberg, and the director decided to share this information with me. And to answer your second question, yes, I think there is a good chance to help. With some accurate treatment and constant observation of Romeo's condition there is an excellent possibility to completely cure him. The medical practice knows a lot of cases where patients with much more severe signs of depression and post traumatic stress were healed totally. And also we need to engage him in some positive activities, for example volunteering for local community or sports programs, to divert his mind's thoughts into a hopeful and encouraging direction. We must help Romeo to start feeling that someone needs him and that he can be of use and that a bright future awaits him."

I said: "Don't you want to do your personal evaluation of the kids' mental state? As I recall director Goldberg would like that. He even authorized using some of the specific skills that you possess on the young gentleman to get better results."

Kristina answered: "That is exactly why I wanted to talk to you. According to my secret source; smart, youthful and beautiful Ena, Romeo spends a lot of time sitting at the bank of the river, watching water flow, birds flying and writing his poetic stories. We can pick him up there, for example tomorrow, and take the young man to one of our safe houses for a hypnosis session."

"This works for me just fine," was my response. Then I looked at my watch and added: "We still have a few minutes before going back to the office and we are not far away from the waterway. Let's drive by and see if our buddy is there, so we would know where to find him tomorrow."

Kristina agreed and we proceeded as was planned. As both of us suspected, Romeo was sitting at one of the benches by the river. We recognized him easily. The kid held a piece of paper in his hands and it looked like he was smiling about something.

The next day, at lunch time, Kristina and I drove by the same place and again we saw our friend sitting at the bench as we did yesterday. This time I stopped the car nearby and we approached Romeo.

Seeing us coming towards him the kid got up from the bench, made an angry face and said: "What do you want?"

Kristina with a very calm voice replied: "Hi Romeo, how are you? We were just passing by and then saw you, so we decided to stop for a moment here and say Hi."

The kid sat back on the bench, saying nothing. He looked very tired and irritated. Dirty clothes and a sleepy facial expression told us that he is in a crisis and needs some rest.

My partner took the initiative in her hands and slowly, step by step, was able to convince Romeo to talk. The young man was like in a slow mode: every time you ask him something, it appeared that the guy was ignoring you and then, after a pause, would come up with an answer. Later Kristina explained to me that those were the signs of his current mental condition. Yes, Romeo recognized us. He even remembered our names: Mr. Chic and Ms. Jones and who we are. It turned out that the kid did not go anywhere since yesterday, he spent the night on the same bench and was really hungry.

While my professional associate was doing her job, persuading Romeo to go with us and promising him good food and rest, I was thinking about those people who put this young gentleman through terrible things. These big boys and girls, meaning adults, played God. They brought the innocent and suspecting nothing kid into their game, and for whatever reason made him a marijuana, alcohol and who knows what else addict. These people did not care that the kid is a human being and that he has a family. They were not concerned with if they hurt somebody or ruined someone's life. My memory brought out the image of a smiling, perfectly healthy little boy, at the age of ten or eleven, sitting in an ideal, one hundred and eighty degree splits, wearing a uniform, practicing Martial Arts. This was a happy kid.

I know what these individuals usually say when they need an excuse to justify their actions. They say: "Nothing personal. I was just doing my job." And I always want to answer: "This, your job, it should not exist at all and it is shitty. Quit it and pray."

In the meanwhile Kristina finished her talk with Romeo and made a sign to me that we can go now. On the way to the safe house, we stopped at one of the many take out restaurants in the area and bought some food for all of us. The young man was eating like a machine, swallowing everything quickly. Sometimes it even looked like he was not chewing... After we satisfied our hunger, I silently disappeared leaving my partner one on one with the client. I did not want to distract any one of them.

Cherry In Liquor

Sometime later, after the hypnosis session when Romeo was asleep in a room, Kristina told me about her findings. She said: "I should thank you for your help and for the opportunity to work with Romeo. He is a very interesting young man. Yes, he seems angry sometimes and he made some poor choices, but those were involuntary choices. Now I can tell for sure that someone worked with him and that person or persons are really skilled at what they do."

I was silently looking at Kristina, waiting for more explanations and she continued: "There is still some potential danger present to Romeo himself and to others, because we do not know yet how the kid was programmed and for what purpose. These behind the scenes people, they can easily manipulate his behavior. As I mentioned earlier, the combination of psychotropic drugs and hypnosis could be very potent. But there is even more. Romeo clearly remembers his time in prison. While he was sitting in a solitary cell or whatever they call it, he believed that some other prisoners in the neighboring cubicle were doing their black magic against him and he felt like various magnetic waves or something else, he can't tell for certain, were going through his head, making him suffer. He thought it was unfriendly inmates; I think otherwise. I suppose that was some high tech equipment aimed to deprive any targeted person of his or her willpower, making them servants. I cannot tell for sure right now, but I know those devices exist and are being used. And I know that a few organizations conduct such illegal experiments on prisoners. Those undisclosed parties, who have appropriate possibilities and resources, as well as most likely unlawful authorizations for such activities from people in power, do whatever they want and they almost always get away with it. In Romeo's case, I accept that it is true that these "normal and average people in everyday life" tested some new technology on prisoners by carrying out dreadful experiments, especially when they knew that they are out of reach of the law and are unseen to the public. Of course there is a possibility that it was something else. We do not know yet, but I will keep digging. With every following session we will be able to receive more and more information and get a better picture of what had happened to the kid."

As Kristina kept moving forward with her clarification of the situation with Romeo, telling me about her latest attention-grabbing discoveries, there were a lot of different thoughts in my head suggesting that it will basically be really difficult to prove anything that has been done to the kid and to find the guilty party responsible for the kid's suffering. Even if we find them, those folks could easily provide some legal authorization papers, such as an informed consent form or something similar, signed by the affected prisoners, clearing those canvassers of any wrong doing. And these "representatives of science" could easily make detainees sign those papers in exchange for food or better living conditions.

In the meantime my partner kept on going: "It is sad that we cannot use both the human and material resources of the Company. If we could, then obviously we would be able to uncover the truth and get the desired results much faster. When I did my session with Romeo, he mentioned eating some sweets. I think he said it was those chocolate covered cherries with liquor inside them. I was not able to find out yet when and under what circumstances Romeo ate the above mentioned candies and why. All I know is that after eating those innocent bonbons he had a vision of his very strict kindergarten teacher with a belt in his arms. The educator appeared from nowhere and with a very angry facial expression made Romeo promise to obey all his orders. Romeo said he was extremely scared of the man; he did not want to be beaten up with the belt and quickly agreed to do as he was told."

Kristina stopped for a moment, looked at me to check my reaction then added: "What do you think?"

I answered: "The use of something common, like chocolate cherries in liquor makes sense if you want to drug someone. It is easy to input some substance within the treat, all you need is a needle to inject "the stuff" into it and moreover, those sweets are delicious."

My smart co-worker nodded her head and said: "You know what is also interesting? To drug a person of interest in that way was a thing of the past. This is an old and well-known technique. Modern methods are more advanced. But anyway, the basic steps are similar: first you create a confused and vulnerable mind, then you program the subject to act in a certain way or to perform a certain task and after that you brainwash the subjects to forget your session with them. They do not remember anything after that, but know their mission. That is why it is very difficult to prove anything or to find the people responsible for the disaster."

I decided to shed some light on Kristina's statement to better understand it and ask her the following: "So, you say that it is an old "modus operandi" and it is somewhat known not to just the professionals, but also to the general public who are educated in this area as well. Then it means it could be any one of the mentioned above: qualified folks or amateurs, interfering for whatever purpose with the life of our young man. Or maybe these unknown people used that method to cover the traces of their deeds and to lead some possible investigation into the wrong direction? Or maybe this was done long ago, when Romeo was still a kid?"

Kristina replied: "It is hard to say right now and to make any conclusions without having enough information. This just proves that we need to ask the director for help and ask for permission to use the agency's resources. Then, I am sure, we will get results quicker. But as I understood correctly, director Goldberg cannot go through the official way. It is an obvious conflict of interests and moreover, it will be difficult to explain to the directors' superiors why we are involved in this case."

I said to Kristina: "I see your point. Let's be creative here. You know better than me that there is always a way to fix the problem and make things right. We just need to look for it. What I suggest: first, we will go and talk to director Goldberg about the situation. He has his own view of the state of affairs regarding this young man and he might be very helpful. Secondly, as I recall, we are expanding, I mean the agency. What if Romeo applies for an entry level position or something similar with the organization, then it gives us a legal ground for checking his background and this matter becomes "our thing". How much time do you think Romeo needs to get back in shape mentally, if he gets proper handling?"

Kristina thought for a moment, then answered: "I already gave Romeo my instructions to return to the hospital for treatment. He will do it tonight, after we are done here. I cannot tell for certain how much time he needs to restore his health; this would depend on the doctor in charge, the prescribed medication and the chosen method to cure him. But my guess is from two to three weeks, maybe a little bit longer, let's say one month, if everything goes well."

I quickly calculated in my head the average job application time, which is about six weeks in many simple cases, and said: "That is exactly the time we need to go through the official way with Romeo, if we make him sign the job application papers in the next few days. But we have to talk to The Goblin initially to get his approval and to discuss with him the position for which Romeo should apply." I stopped for a split second, looked at my watch, then at Kristina, she nodded her head agreeing with me and then I continued: "It is about time for us to return to the office, do you want to wake Romeo up? I think we can drive him to the hospital. He gave me the impression of being very tired."

Kristina replied: "He should feel much better now, subsequent to the hypnosis session, but I think it is a good idea to take him there, just to be sure that everything is fine and according to the plan."

After Romeo appeared in the room, I noticed that his facial expression had changed. It still had the traces of sleepiness on it, but his eyes were looking at you in a different manner, more relaxed and friendly. Somehow the young man was hungry again and he had asked for food right away. I thought it is a good indication of a significant improvement in his health and that he gets better, because a person usually wants to eat when they are well. My partner quickly reacted on Romeo's request and brought him some food. When our patient was done with it, we took him back to the hospital, to the emergency department. Later that day I called to the medical facility to double check if Romeo was admitted there and a nice and polite lady on the other end of the line confirmed just so.

Five minutes before the end of the day Kristina and I met with director Goldberg in his headquarters. We briefly informed The Goblin about the situation with Romeo and asked the director the following. Kristina said: "Sir, I came across numerous resistances when working with our client, trying to find out what happened to him, was it accidental or not and if anything has been done on purpose. And today I can say with confidence, I am ninety nine point nine percent sure that someone worked with Romeo. And that someone has skills. They did everything to cover their traces. Today we have many questions such as why, when, for what purpose, who is behind it, and so on. And we do not have answers. If we keep digging for the truth with the same pace, it might take a while to get into the kid's head and to discover that hidden clue. But if we use our Company's resources, then obviously we will be able to speed up the process. And as I understand time is very important. Also, I am aware that we must stay discreet and not to show that we are involved in this matter. It means we cannot ask our colleagues for help. Like my partner says there is always a way to make things right if you look for it. What if we bring Romeo to the agency as an employee? I remember we already talked about that. And you Sir mentioned that the business is mounting."

The Goblin patiently and with full attention listened to what Kristina said and then replied: "Yes, I remember our conversation and I already talked to HR. You can bring the kid in as the Field Agent Trainee. We have a few positions open and that one is yours. Please help this young man with his resume, the cover letter and go with him through the whole application process. You should instruct Romeo on what to say and when and how to behave himself during the interview. Explain to the man what things to look forward to and what is expected of him. And as soon as Romeo is here, at least officially on paper, then you can start using the agency's resources and work with your associates to get the desired results. Also, once again, I would like to thank both of you for doing a great job."

The next few days Kristina and I were busy with our regular employment duties, periodically monitoring Romeo's health status over the phone by calling the hospital and speaking to him. Every day the young man sounded better and better. His answers were faster and more to the point. Good rest, proper medication and fine food played its part. During this period of time at the office I did not forget to talk to the HR person, a very nice and smart lady, who confirmed having a conversation with the director about the position of a Field Agent Trainee and she gave me the green light to bring the kid in.

One afternoon, when we had a little window in our schedule, Kristina and I went to the hospital to see Romeo. This time we had the job application papers with us; and of course we brought him some food. Somehow big boys usually feel happier when they see tasty groceries available to them and our patient was not an exception to this rule, on the opposite, we could call him the founder.

The department of mental health, into which Romeo got placed this time, was located at the top floor of the hospital building. The entrance doors to the facility were locked all the time and there were security cameras everywhere. Also, you have to sign in with the nurse on duty, before you are allowed into the section where the patient is. And evidently they, the staff associates, will check the possessions that visitors bring in for their friends and family members, who happened to be going through difficult times and were admitted to the division dealing with psychological problems. Romeo, as everyone else, had his own private room. The room was not that big in size, but large enough to place in there a bed, a table and a book shelf. In addition to the already mentioned manufactured goods, there was a diminutive cabinet for the patient's clothes at one of the corners of the cubicle. The entrance door to the compartment had a glass window in it, so the medical professionals could easily check the condition of their patients.

Our good friend was in his booth, laying in the bed and reading one of the books he had. Romeo looked great. He was shaved, clean, well rested and in a good mood. Actually he gave the impression of being much younger without a beard. Like maybe five, six years younger. I had a very pleasant feeling seeing Romeo like this. You, as a good citizen, are always happy to see someone you know getting better, both physically and emotionally.

When we knocked on his door, the young man got up quickly and greeted us like his old friends, saying: "Nice to see you people again. What brought you here this time?"

Kristina answered: "We decided to visit you to check

on your health status and we need to talk to you about something important as well."

The chap did not look surprised with my partner's words. He hurriedly went outside of the room and returned back in a brief second, bringing in a chair from the corridor. The other chair, similar to the new one, was already in the cubicle. After that Romeo offered us to sit and jumped on his bed, ready to listen. I put the bag with food I had in my hands on the table and decided to ask my youthful friend about his personal plans for his future saying the following: "I noticed you are getting better and probably will be out of here soon. What is next? Do you want to go back to school or do you want to start working?"

The young man replied: "I was thinking of joining the Army. We had a conversation here with some folks and doctors recently and I figured out that it will be a good idea for me to become a military man. And the pay is good and there are other benefits. What do you think?" And he looked at me waiting for an answer. Kristina too, smiling politely, added: "What do you think?"

I said: "I honestly believe it is a good idea, if you see yourself in the Armed Forces. Also, I want to warn you that it is not easy to join the Army; you have to have a high school diploma and pass a number of different tests. And I think having a driver's license will definitely help as well. Obviously you can learn a lot in the Army and turn into a stronger and better person. But today I want you to consider some other options to be useful to society. For example being a Firefighter or serving as a Police Officer."

Romeo reacted right away: "They would not let me serve in Law Enforcement; I made a few bad choices."

This time Kristina decided to interfere: "You are

still very young and can easily change your life. What is important is that you understand that those were poor decisions you made. And as soon as you know the problem, you can fix it."

Romeo said nothing in response to my partner's statement; he was just sitting there on his bed, smiling and thinking about something unknown to us. In the meantime I continued: "I see your point, but we are here to offer you something different. How about a position with some powerful organization, which requires a combination of skills needed in the Army, in the Police and so on and moreover it is an opportunity for you to serve your country as well."

The young man made a serious face and looked at me initially, then at Kristina and answered: "Do you want me to become an astronaut? Or do you have something else in mind?"

I replied: "Of course I do; otherwise why would I bring it up?" Kristina pulled out a piece of paper with the description of the available job duties and said: "Here is the vacancy we would like you to consider." And she handed the paper to Romeo, then continued: "It is a very interesting and well paid opportunity for someone young, smart and strong like you are. With this job you will have the possibility to learn a lot and to utilize the skills you possess already. First, if you accept the offer, you will have to go through the extensive training for a certain period of time, where you would not have much chance to sleep at all; most likely three to four hours per day on average. Then, if you pass all the required tests and your superiors see that you are prepared for the next level, you will start working in the Field, carrying out more complex assignments. And after that, when you are absolutely ready, you will become a valuable part of a team of the great professionals. How does this sound?"

Romeo carefully looked at the paper, reading every single line in it and answered: "Sounds remarkable, but there is a lot of stuff here in this document, which I do not have on my resume."

Now it was my turn to speak and I said: "That is right. I like your honesty. And that is why this opening is called A Trainee position. You will have the chance to add all the missing information to your resume going through the schooling. I want you to look at it that way; I want you to be confident in your abilities. You have a lot to put forward. For example: your Martial Arts skills. Not that many people are at your level; even if you include in this list the very well trained Martial Artists. And moreover, you are an intelligent young man and a bright future is ahead of you. We do not want to push you to make the decision today. We want you to think of it for a few days and then we will continue our conversation. Also, I would like to ask you to stay discreet. You can talk about this job offer with your family members, but no one else please. And do not worry; we will help you go through the whole application process and training if you decide to apply for this apprenticeship position."

After a brief pause, the young man agreed to think concerning all of that. He even promised to start working out again as soon as he gets better. This was a good sign for us. We spent another ten minutes with our client asking him treatment related questions: what type of medication does he take? How many times per day? And so on. Romeo did not know much. He said he takes only one pill per day, which his doctor gives him every morning and he does not even know the name of the pill. When we were leaving the facility, we asked the nurse on duty about Romeo and for how long they plan to keep him in the department. The nurse replied that she cannot provide this information because she is not allowed, but remembered overhearing Romeo's doctor mention that the kid needs a time period of at least a few weeks to heal completely.

A DELICATE MATTER

When you are really busy, the time is passing by very quickly. It has been a few days by now since we talked to Romeo. And as we promised to the young man, Kristina and I had already scheduled our next visit to the hospital for tomorrow, to continue the job related talks with him. But today, as soon as I showed up at the office, director Goldberg called me into his headquarters immediately. He knew that I was going to be late at work that day, due to the involvement I had with the undercover activities of my other colleagues. We are a good team and we help each other.

When I entered the directors' study, apart from him there were two other persons in the room. One of them was previously well known to me, Mr. Mark Donovan, the representative of some Diplomatic Service or something similar and the other man was a popular politician, whom I saw on TV many times before. The director went first: "Serge, please meet Mr. Bureau and Mr. Donovan here does not need any introduction to you; you had a chance to work with him before."

I quickly greeted Mr. Donovan by saying: "Nice to meet you Sir," and then introduced myself to the elected official. The man wanted to say something to me in return, but The Goblin took the initiative into his hands and with a very happy voice said: "Good news Serge. After spending about two weeks in prison, your friends John Kalger and Rebecca Lung will be released from custody soon. The negotiations continued for a while, but eventually the agreement was reached."

I replied: "It is good news. Do you know any more details Sir?"

Director Goldberg looked at Mr. Donovan like inviting him to come forward and responded: "Mr. Donovan here has more information."

The diplomat thought for a moment, then delivered his short ambassadorial speech: "As it usually happens in circumstances like that, one side has threatened the other with economical sanctions, political scandals, international attention to the matter and so on. And of course the other side had their own counter arguments. But in reality both parties were just trying to resolve the issue by getting as much as possible from the transaction. Eventually they found the way to deal with the affair and your friends will be free soon. Most likely the countries involved in the disagreement will exchange something for something: for example a person for a person, or persons for business opportunities and so on. Anyway, today it should not concern us much who will exchange whom and for what. All I can tell you is that we are very happy with the outcome of the whole thing and our best and reliable people are coming home in a little while."

This time addressing to Mr. Mark Donovan I said: "It is really good news. Thank you Sir."

As soon as the civil servant stopped explaining the details of the successful maneuver done by our clever representatives, the director, who still wanted to stay in control over the conversation, stepped in by saying: "This is not all, Serge. We have another issue for you to deal with. As you probably figured out by now Mr. Bureau here is a very well known political heavyweighter and he is present at the moment at this office for a reason. Mr. Bureau wants to talk to you about some delicate matter. He came to us for help and Mr. Donovan and I, after learning all the aspects of the subject, recommended you as the most tactful and qualified agent. And of course you will need some assistance of your colleagues, especially technical staff, to fix everything, and I am giving you permission to cooperate with your coworkers on the topic, but I want you to stay discreet. No names, no leads, no anything. Is it clear?"

I answered: "Yes Sir, I will do my best as usual."

After that director Goldberg turned to the politician and said: "Please Mr. Bureau, go ahead."

The elected official, with the same confident facial expression as he had on his face all this time, said: "I am sure you have heard previously about the so called DSS or the decision support system. I am not talking about marketing tricks here, which store managers use to help people to buy commodities. I am talking about something else. In my interpretation the decision support system is an out of the ordinary scheme, when a player or a team of players often unlawfully force their opponent or opponents to make a certain move or decision or to cooperate with them on some unethical business." Then Mr. Bureau paused for a short period of time, examining my reaction to his words. I even thought for a brief moment that such type of behavior: confidence, establishing good contact with your audience, making sure that your message is delivered and so on, is probably a part of his job. And I replied: "Yes Sir, I know DSS. In our line of work we use it periodically too. And moreover, sometimes we find it helpful."

Satisfied with my answer the story teller continued: "These faceless people, they have something on anyone or almost anyone, who happened to be visible, even slightly. If the person's social status or position produces an interest to those nameless individuals, then they will find something embarrassing about that personage. If these anonymous people do not have anything on the person of interest, then they will create uncomfortable stuff. As you know, especially in politics, sometimes even a little rumor is enough to ruin someone's career..."

I listened carefully to every word said by Mr. Bureau, trying to understand the direction into which he was going. The man gave the impression that he was honest in telling his fairy-tale, but so far the elected official was rolling around, not releasing any details yet. I even thought that those politicians are like Intelligence Agents: clever, careful, enigmatic and good looking. You can drop the "good looking" part, because everyone considers themselves to be just that. Anyway, Mr. Bureau continued: "I have a family. And your family is your fortress; it gives you happiness and delight, energy and motivation and much-much more. But it is also your responsibility to protect your loved ones. One day, a long time ago, when I started moving forward with my career, I noticed some unusual activity around myself and my family. Those were previously unknown to me people, who later pretended to be my friends. I am not the smartest guy out there, but eventually I realized that those were the "creators". These people tried to learn everything about me and my family. They were looking for any opportunity to find any faults or wrongdoings and get something, which they could probably use later as leverage against me, to lobby their interests. After I became conscious regarding all of this, I understood that if they, these people, would not find anything humiliating, then, most likely, they will create stuff and they might even use my family members to try to harm me. And this is another territory, a dangerous one. You do not want your loved ones to be involved in something like this and to suffer. What do you do in situations like that? Obviously I could not fight them without having any proof of anything. So, I decided to play along."

All of us, director Goldberg, Mr. Donovan and I, listened carefully, paying full attention to what was said. Eventually, despite the political correctness of Mr. Bureau, I started getting the picture. I even thought that this is not the first time I came across a story like this. We had to deal with a few similar cases before.

In the meanwhile the speaker continued: "You know, when two boxers fight each other and they are both good, but one is slightly better, the better one could see when the other boxer is going to attack. So, he strikes first, just before his opponent. I used the same strategy. I threw my punches a little bit earlier than the opposition. I did it to protect my family. These people set up an appropriate situation and as a result I took a part in the adult movie. It happened just once and I want to emphasize: I was protecting my family," after these last words Mr. Bureau looked at me like trying to understand my reaction.

And I said: "Sir, we do not judge." Then added: "Do you have any names, hints or other information, which could be useful, such as phone numbers or the name of the business and so on?"

Mr. Bureau reached into his pocket and pulled out a piece of paper. "Here," he said. "This is the full report. I wrote down all the details: dates, the name of the company, phone and fax numbers. I knew I might need it one day," and he handed his notes to me. I thought "how nice". I would consider it "a lot" already, having just the phone number. But I had more than that. Anyway, the politician carried on addressing to me: "Of course you, as the man in charge of this matter, want to know as much as possible to determine better ways to deal with all of these human slip-ups. Well, here is everything that had happened. Since it is a legit business and not a homemade amateur movie, I had to go to the medical clinic first to pass a certain amount of tests in order to show the organizers that I am healthy. When I got the results, I faxed it to the number you have on that piece of paper. A couple of days later someone from their organization called me on my phone with directions, the address of the hotel, it is written down too, and the time at which I should be there. I showed up at the specified place as instructed and in a few hours the embarrassing moment was over. I knew after the incident that these people are going to leave me and my family alone for a while. Their goal was achieved. I gave them what they wanted and now they have something on me too. And you would not believe me if I tell you that everything had happened exactly as I suspected. In some short period of time those individuals, so called "friends", silently disappeared from my horizon the same way as they had appeared previously."

Probably Mr. Mark Donovan wanted to be supportive to his companion, because he suddenly interfered into the conversation and said: "We know each other for many years already. You, my friend, despite your high status, are just a simple man. If, for whatever reason, that thing goes public, you still have a chance to turn this unfortunate event to your advantage with the help of the right people and a proper campaign."

The politician replied: "Right now I am thinking about my kids and my family. I do not want them to get upset. And as I mentioned earlier, I did this to protect them. I am sure you understand. And moreover, I do not create rules, they, these mysterious folks, they do. But I play by the rules. I have to. Because, as I stated previously, if you do not play by the rules, then someone might get hurt and I do not want that to happen."

I was listening to the words said by Mr. Bureau, at the same time reasonably thinking "if this is true, which it almost certainly is, then who might be behind all of that? Is it some criminal union or business boys? Or do they work together? Or maybe this was an unknown third party, similar to our organization? Everything is possible. Today we do not have the answers, but time will tell."

Now it was the director's turn to say something. Who could possibly know more about the rules than the man in charge of the Intelligence Agency himself? The Goblin said: "We live in a society. And that society lives by the rules. I agree. But there are always those individuals or groups of people who constantly break the rules or create their own. All we can do and need to do in situations like this is to simply outplay those criminals. And we have all the resources and everything else to accomplish just that."

Mr. Bureau reacted: "Thank you, director, for your support and understanding. I hope this delicate matter will be resolved soon."

While listening to all those exchanges of pleasantries and assurances by serious people, I already started the investigation in my head and asked the elected official the following: "Sir, did you receive any threats or did anyone get in touch with you recently regarding the sensitive business discussed herein?"

The man replied: "No, thank God, no." Then he gratefully looked up at the ceiling and added: "As I mentioned earlier I think it is not wise to wait for something horrific to happen. I have played sports since my childhood and have learned a few things. I am trying to use the preventive measures first and like a good boxer land my punches before the opposition even thinks to throw theirs. If the matter goes public, then it means I refused to be a doll in someone's hands. The situation becomes unpredictable and might turn in any direction. As Mark said previously, with the right campaign and first-class people we may twist this thing around and still get some advantage out of it. But what if anything goes wrong? Then it means I have to resign and let down a lot of good citizens, which is not acceptable."

I said: "I understand your point Sir. Please correct me if I am wrong, but the way I see it, all we need to do is secretly find all the copies of that movie and destroy them. Is that not right? In this scenario no one knows that you are involved and made a move. I suggest we wipe out not just a single video clip, but the whole bunch of them pertaining to a certain period of time, let's say six months or one year. As it is clear to me now the business is legit and almost certainly they have all the proper documentation to keep the tax and government guys away. And if this is the case, then it might take a while to find some faults in their system, if we decide to go through the official way. Of course we would not mention your name and the real purpose of our interest in this company, if we try to shut them down. And also this bureaucratic approach would not guarantee that they, these nameless people, do not have some copies of the video hidden in a safe place."

The politician answered: "One head is good, but two is better. I like your way of thinking. You have already found a simple solution: no real facts against me; means that no problem exists."

Director Goldberg said calmly: "Let's say the evidence was destroyed. And if someone still tries to contact you and make you play by their rules, then most likely they are bluffing. In this case you can use the available resources of the Police to stop those criminals, but we have to be one hundred percent sure that all the evidence was destroyed."

At this point of our conversation my thoughts were going in all directions, searching for the right and best strategy to solve the mystery and I asked Mr. Bureau the next question: "Sir, do you remember the type of video equipment those folks used while shooting the movie? It is important."

The man scratched his head, probably going back to the event in his memory and replied: "I think it was a 35 mm professional camera with a microphone and all accessories. I recall that someone talked about the equipment they use and they claimed it to be professional and modern, but again this was in the past, years ago. You have the dates."

I decided to clarify the information and added: "Was it just one camera or more? Did they use any still photo equipment as well?"

The elected official responded quickly: "No, it was just one camera, nothing else."

I got all the information I needed from the man and before leaving the room I said: "Sir, I am not giving you my business card because it is not safe. You are a public figure and if someone from the opposite camp accidentally sees it, then they might pull the alarm, causing unwanted commotion or may get the wrong idea reading something between the lines, which is not there. And if you need to contact me or happen to remember any additional details, please use the director's channel to pass the info on."

After that we said good bye to each other and I left. Not wasting any time I went straight to our tech support team. These guys are big professionals, experts. They have many useful tricks in their storage. One of the specialists named Gordon was a friend of mine. Not giving him any extra information I asked Gordon to pull up all the reports on the company in question. Also, I told him that The Goblin wants all the video files for the specified year, belonging to that organization, to be destroyed or become unusable, without leaving any traces. And of course I asked Gordon about the best way to do the job. The man knew what to do. He quickly found all the information requested. The owner of the company was a very interesting lady. She, for whatever reason, altered her name a few times. Women, when they get married, usually change their last names, but the first name stays the same. In our case the lady changed her first name two times. She had a previous criminal record for fraudulent activity, but somehow managed to stay atop. Probably she had powerful friends or big money played its part. Obviously this lady was paranoid, trusted no one, with the exception of her boyfriend/ personal assistant/security guard, with whom she lived at the address the computer genius found on her file.

Gordon said: "We should not have any problems destroying the videos which are remote accessible. But I am sure you understand that there is a good possibility that certain files were copied and stored at a protected place somewhere else."

I replied: "I know, thank you. Do you have any recommendations?"

Smiling politely Gordon answered: "We should engage our "Bear" team in this operation. If The Goblin wants the job done perfectly, then we need their assistance. Those guys are like ghosts; they can get into a hostile diplomatic mission unnoticed, which is not easy already by its definition, open any safe, copy the documents and get out of there without being detected. They are that good, because if they get caught, then it is an international scandal and I do not recall any events like that for the past while, throwing a shadow at us or suggesting our involvement."

Later that night, around three thirty in the morning, like TV criminals dressed all in black and wearing masks, we broke into the office of that company. There were three of us; two "Bear" team boys: "Fox" and "Jackal" and I. These men; they do not use their real names while communicating with each other. They go by nicknames. They called me "Giraffe" for this operation. Why "Giraffe"? Maybe because this animal is big and can see further, I do not know. Gordon was at his workplace, providing us with the technical support, shutting down the security cameras in the neighborhood and watching for some other unwanted activities in the area, monitoring the surroundings.

The building's protection system did not cause any trouble at all. It was a "piece of cake" for my companions. We had all the necessary gear, including firearms and night vision goggles. No one cancelled yet the "always be prepared" principle. The company's office was quite large in size. It had a reception area, where one of the computers was located.

Actually they, the owners of this company, had computers in almost every room, a total seven of them. What is also interesting, they had security cameras in each office space, including the reception. It was a clear sign proving the fact that the owner of the business does not trust anyone and wants to stay in control of things every single moment. Also, they had quite an interesting and very well decorated basement. Two big beds separated by a curtain were in there. It looked like they used that space for shooting movies as well. It did not take us much time to find the storage area, where we found eleven external memory devices. Two video cameras were in the basement and five more upstairs. The cameras were relatively new, maximum three years old. Anyway, we checked them too. One hour later our job at that location was done. As I suspected the database contained the files with the names of people: in the last name, dot, and first name format. It is reasonable because this structure makes it easier to search for a specific video that way. While doing the job we came for, I copied a number of files for our own sake. I knew that The Goblin would not understand me if I did not. He likes to say: "Always have something to use as leverage when dealing with different sorts of people." It does not mean that he is going to use that embarrassing video against or to the advantage of the big politician, who, by the way, came to him for help and for our director friendship means friendship, but I had to do what I had to do in order to finish the job at hand. I was not going to pass the copied information to the director just yet anyway, unless he asked me to.

"Fox" and "Jackal" worked very professionally. Their moves were so smooth, quick and effortless, I even thought while watching them doing their tricks that they spend a lot of time practicing this stuff and learning new things and systems. That is how you stay in shape. We did not touch anything we were not supposed to and if we did, we left the equipment the same way as it was before. Even the dust was left where it should have been.

After our job was done at this location, Gordon did his. All the targeted videos were destroyed, corrupted or deleted. But that was not all. We had to do a few more things. When the paranoid lady and her boyfriend left their place of residence for work, we decided to pay a visit to her well protected empty apartment. The fact that the woman does not trust anyone played its part. My team members did not believe that she does not have some stash in the form of a memory card or an external hard drive or similar, hidden in a safety deposit box or we can use another word for it: in a high tech safe.

When we, with the help of our eyes and ears named Mr. Gordon, approached the apartment's entrance door, "Fox" raised his arm and showed us that the door was sealed. Yes sealed. Sealed by the owner. It was just a little, tiny piece of a match placed in between the door and the door frame. Very smart. If you open the door, the piece of the match falls on the floor and when the owner returns they can see that the door was opened in their absence and someone was inside the apartment. Also, as it turned out, these people had a pretty advanced alarm system on their premises. And that was not all. "Fox" and "Jackal" quickly found a couple of hidden video cameras activated by motion sensors. Seeing all of this I even thought "Who is this lady? An obsessed foolish person or an experienced conspirator?" Anyway, as we have suspected, the safe, which was located behind the curtain in the master bedroom, contained a few external memory devices, some jewelry and a significant amount of cash. "Jackal" opened it faster than one could even imagine. And sometimes you wonder why good citizens pay that much money for something which could be opened that quickly. I always suggest to my friends to keep their hard earned currency in a bank. Let the bank worry how to protect your fortune. We did not touch the money and ornaments, just went through the contents of the memory gadgets, found what we were looking for, destroyed the files and put everything back in the same way as it was before. Our goal was not to rob these folks, but to wipe out the embarrassing evidence, which could possibly ruin the life of a good and honest person, a public servant, who got into that undesirable situation, believing that he was protecting his family. This just proves that even big politicians are humans and do controversial stuff. You may question his chosen method, but have to respect the wish of that man to keep his loved ones protected. Also, there were two more personal computers in the apartment, but the specified file was not found in each one of them.

While telling you about our adventure in the apartment of our "clients", I almost forgot to mention the fact that when the paranoid lady and her boyfriend were leaving their place of residence in the morning, going to work, The Goblin already sent a surveillance team after them. This was done in order to monitor their activities and reactions for the next couple of days in case they happened to discover that someone paid a visit to their home and office. We did not want any surprises and wanted to be sure that our job was done at the highest level possible.

Later that day, when I was briefing the director on the subject, he asked me the following. The Goblin said: "You copied the files, did you not?"

I answered: "Yes, I did."

"Delete the one with our customer and keep the rest of them. I am sure there might be more bombshells, maybe not at the same level, but powerful enough to sabotage someone's life or blackmail somebody for money," continued the director.

Again I answered: "Understood, will do it."

Shortly after our meeting with director Goldberg, as I promised to him I deleted the "political" file. Maybe it was a mistake, but that was the right thing to do. We are professional average people, honest and loyal to our values, who happened to be in the position to do their job by helping others.

While I was busy performing certain urgent and delicate tasks, keeping myself outside of the office for some time, Kristina went to the hospital by herself to visit Romeo, as we promised to the young man. She had all the job related papers with her as well. When later that day Kristina saw me at the office, she said: "I have good news. Romeo is getting better. When I arrived at the hospital today, he was not there. The nurse on duty told me that he got a day pass or something similar, meaning he left the facility in the morning and should be back in the evening. The nurse said they give those day passes to patients who feel better and are on the road to recovery. Since it was not clear what time Romeo was coming back to the hospital, I decided to reschedule our visit, but now I know that we have to call first, to make sure he is there."

I replied: "Good, very good. Let's go and visit him in the near future, as soon as we have free time and the kid is at the facility, but you are right, we have to call first to make sure he is there."

My Cases

With all that running around and doing extracurricular activities, to an untrained eye it might look like I forgot about my regular job duties, the very dearest other projects I am working on. Let me assure you: I have not. And I think it is the time to tell you about my primary assignments, on some of which I am operating for a long period of time by now.

In our line of duty the new tasks could come in every day. It does not matter if you feel that you are getting too much of a load or if you are very busy already with something equally important. You cannot say no. The lives of the people could depend on you. Always be prepared mentally and physically to do the job. Understand the matter and what is required, analyze the situation, set goals and priorities, multitask, delegate responsibilities, be a team player and a solo performer at the same time. Yes, sometimes you have to take a risk, but with the proper preparation the risk you take could be manageable. You can control the risk. And what is also vital, do not be afraid to solicit for help if you really need it and do not refuse to help others, if you are asked to do so. When you do all the mentioned above and execute your missions step by step, eventually you will get the desired results and the satisfaction of knowing the fact that your job was very well done. Moreover, you will be surprised how far you have advanced with your projects over a certain period of time.

Anyway, let me return to my cases. I am going to present the information in the received order and not in the order of importance. Case number one:

A few months ago our partner agency, the Counter Intel boys, asked for our assistance with some interesting investigation of possible fraudulent activities, going around one legally registered company. Let's name this corporation "Artscam". The companionship under suspicion had all the proper documentation; they paid all the required taxes on time and did not have any complaints or law cases against them. The business had its head office in our country, but they worked internationally, supplying high tech microchips to their intercontinental collaborators. The scheme they used was simple and yet complicated. Those high tech double purpose microchips are used in military and in general environments and are very difficult to produce. The Government, to eliminate the possibility of doubtful organizations getting the mechanisms, included these costly devices into the so called "trading restrictions list", prohibiting its sale to the parties in question. In reality, only a few friendly countries were allowed to buy the gear, if you want me to be totally honest. The unknown people behind the "Artscam", we had to find out who they are, created a few businesses in the countries, which are our allies and the trade went on. No need to mention that it was multimillion commerce. After the gadgets were out of the country, the people involved in the plot resold these devices to the third parties, who were often located in the countries to which the trade was prohibited. To trace the whole chain and to figure out how we can turn the situation to our advantage was our mission. There were a few possible scenarios. We could simply shut the business down, proving the fact that their activities are unlawful. And eventually we will do that. But today, there are some other options, for example to sell the same microchips, only slightly adjusted in quality, to the same players. And who knows what will happen next with the equipment into which these adjusted gadgets were placed.

This whole investigation required a lot of resources and time; we had to monitor the activities of that organization and its people not just domestically, but all around the world as well. We needed to know what our opposition is up to. If those devices are used for military purposes, then it means that innocent people might suffer. It means danger. At the same time a group of lawyers paid by the Counter Intel people or whoever else, were looking at the matter, trying to understand which charges to bring. If it were just criminal actions by greedy scammers, then it is a different situation from the one involving a threat to the National security. But in order to determine the course of action we needed information. And that is exactly what I was trying to do. I was one of the professionals, mixed up in the case, going after the facts. Sometimes I worked on this assignment a few hours per day, sitting by the computer at my desk, sometimes less. And occasionally I had to travel abroad to meet with our people to double check the info and to execute other tasks.

The new tasks come and go and every now and then you are able to find the answers to the questions you have in front of you, sometimes during a short period of time, like two or three days, and sometimes it takes much longer. This second case that I am working on is very time consuming, complicated and requires scrupulous work, but it is worth it. Let me explain. As everyone knows it's not difficult to move a piece of paper from one side of the table to the other when you sit at your desk and work with documents. When you deal with actual people, some of which are real character individuals, it is, if truth be told, totally different. Attach to it credentials with security features and you will see what I am talking about. My next assignment necessitates cloak-and-dagger work with the personnel of some diplomatic missions to get access to the specific information regarding the authenticity of passports and other legal and travel documents of those countries for our agents. You want to do the best job possible because you know your friends and coworkers must feel confident and secure when using fake, but at the same time "real" IDs. And with some of these identification papers you can move freely to almost any place in the world.

Of course it requires a lot of preparation, research and analysis to identify the right person whom you can approach with such an offer, a business proposition, which they cannot refuse. Everything has its price. And sometimes to catch that person of interest into your net you just have to find something in their past, present, or everyday life or it could even be a suitable character trait. For example: gambling or money problems, feelings of being underappreciated or underpaid, love for luxury, jealousy, anger and so on. And occasionally, when the situation requires, you create that press-stud yourself, with the help of others. Also, it is very important to keep in mind that you are not alone, you might not be the only one interested in that particular person. Most likely the security staff or Counter Intelligence boys of that diplomatic mission will be monitoring the unusual activities of their employees. In addition to that do not count out other parties, such as Foreign Intelligence Services (FIS), criminal elements and business people. Some FIS can easily trade you in if it is in their interests. It is very important to think through the secure ways of exchanging the information with your asset and almost certainly you will have to pay for that info. The price must be correct and appropriate. Make sure you are not being played and what you got is real and authentic. It takes time and resources to validate the received data, but this should be the first thing you do. The whole chain of the operation must be reliable, self-sufficient and simple. Yes, simple. Something uncomplicated always leaves you with less chance to make an error.

When I was facing the above mentioned task initially, I decided to take a closer look at some unsuspicious and less ambitious diplomatic missions abroad, not in our country. And now you know why. After I got the first results, I volunteered to test the new information myself and see how it works in practice, but director Goldberg said that I am too valuable for a pretty straightforward mission like that. Instead of me The Goblin sent two other persons to travel abroad: one was the observer with the totally legal documentation and the other one was the tester, who used the new phony passport. Every time that the tester showed his ID, while crossing the border or somewhere else, the observer was nearby secretly watching the whole process and the reactions of the officials. Everything went very well the first time, but we needed to do more various trials in different countries and extra time to carry out that task, as well as new information for better analysis.

The third case I have in my store is slightly unusual,

if such a definition does exist in someone's vocabulary, but the matter requires the full effort from my side and careful consideration by some other specialists, who have the specific knowledge of the Directed Energy Weapons (DEWs). The DEWs are the types of devices which use electromagnetic radiation to deliver mechanical or electrical energy, heat and so on, to a certain target to cause a variety of special effects. And sometimes those effects are really harmful and occasionally are very subtle. These DEWs can be used against military targets, humans and electronic equipment, depending on the technology and the intentions of the user.

I was appointed to work this case because director Goldberg decided so. Maybe he thinks I am the best guy for the job? Anyway, it was brought to our attention recently that a few "strange and bizarre" incidents had happened in one of the so called developed countries. Let's name that country "country A". The smart and attentive people from one of our departments, who keep an eye on global affairs, stumbled upon a controversial story, which caught their attention. What is important, the information received came from some other country, which belongs to the same "developed countries" niche. Let's name this second country "country B". It was an interesting article in one of the "country B's" local newspapers claiming that a few high ranked professional sportsmen of "country B", while competing at a high level sports event, which took place in "country A", were affected by some unknown power. This unidentified power, out of the blue, made the athletes weak and fragile and as a result their performance led to a fiasco. The debatable article was written by a couple of psychologists who are well known to the local people, and work with professional athletes, various contestants and such. We decided to take a closer look at the situation because not long ago one of our VIP (Very Important Person) officials visited "country A" on business and later the reports came in from the bodyguards of that bureaucrat and other members of the delegation stating the fact that some of them suddenly got puny and sick during the visit. First, everyone tried to blame the food, but after careful consideration of all the known factors, the "food version" was put away. This new "distant impact" theory, involving the high tech devices, presented by the psychologists, could turn the whole investigation into a totally new direction. What if, hypothetically speaking, somehow someone used one of those electromagnetic radiation weapons, which are a type of Directed Energy Weapons and secretly tested something harmful on these people? As I was told by our specialists there are different types of those weapons and some of them are high-energy radio frequency weapons (HERF) and high-power radio frequency weapons (HPRF), which are used to disrupt electronics, and also there are high and low power pulsed microwave devices employing low-frequency radiation. And that low-frequency radiation has similar characteristics, such as frequencies and amplitudes, as human brain waves have. It is not a secret that the lungs, heart, and other vital organs are precisely controlled by very low voltage electric signals from the human brain. It should be possible not just in theory, but in practice too, to disrupt, disastrously, such signals from a certain distance using this technology. Of course we have to ask ourselves those sorts of questions: Who would do that and for what purpose? And so on... Also, we need to take into consideration the possibility of a third party involvement. All the occurrences had happened in the same country, which is the clear sign of the potential contribution to the happenings of some or other local parties. But it could easily be someone else, for example a "country C". If anything appalling happens and the information spreads out and becomes available to the public, then everyone would blame "country A". It will be difficult to link "country C" to the events. But again, it is all just assumptions and theories. We need more facts, information and time to check these suppositions.

Case number four that I am working on relates to the Intel on secure communications between aircraft and ground stations or between aircraft stations. We are particularly interested in the new designed technique of efficient secure communication for aero wireless networks. This innovative technology was created by the specialists of one of the military oriented countries and we need to know what they are up to. Also, our goal is to find out if these well educated and smart people from that country came up with the innovative idea themselves or was it done with the help of others? It is very important to establish the truth because we have something similar in use by our Military and if it was a leakage of information on our side, we need to catch the traitor. When director Goldberg asked me on the phone to come to his office, I heard some other voices in the background, so I knew The Goblin was not alone. After I knocked on the door and received permission to enter, I saw three visitors who were unknown to me; two men and one lady. First, the director introduced me to the lady, who turned out to be a representative of the Counter Intelligence Agency. I thought to myself that even though I am not new in the business and know many people from that organization, I never met her before. Then he introduced me to the men. One of the visitors was strange and an unusual looking gentleman dressed in a black suite with brown colored shoes on his feet and a very bright tie and he was from some research and development (R&D) institution. The other man represented the Military; he was not dressed in the uniform, but you can tell right away that he is Military just by looking at his short haircut, big jaw, and confident demeanor. After the formal introduction The Goblin said: "Serge, I have another assignment for you. I want you to look at it as not just your regular job, but a special mission, an opportunity to kill two birds with one stone. Our colleagues and partners here came to us for help and that is exactly what we are going to do."

I replied: "Sir, anything we do uses the kill two or more birds with one stone strategy. Whatever it is I will do my best as usual."

The director and each other member of our little amalgamation briefly told me about the case, explained their concerns and pointed out the desired direction into which I should move to make my services effective. Also, the kill two birds with one stone approach in the understanding of my collaborators presumed the following: getting new Intel on the subject matter is one bird, and the other bird is the detection of probable leakage of secret know-how by our side. All the involved parties agreed to appoint me as the leading man on this issue and promised every possible help, which included human and material resources as well as information support. I was happy to work this case because I could learn a lot. Sometimes you get really surprised at how these creative people, especially the ones from the R&D institutions, come up with such ideas as the interception of encrypted data and the insertion of new "reliable" data instead in communication channels. Or another ingenious and wild idea of killing the Global Positioning System (GPS) signals on enemies' airplanes. While moving forward on working this complicated matter I came across one technological solution, which learning about made me impressed the most. That complex machine was specifically designed to keep an eye on the protection of information and assessment of electro-magnetic environment. The appliance is capable not just of detecting the position of radio-electronic means and their characteristics, but shutting down the channels of possible information outflow as well. Over the period of time functioning on this high tech affair I was able to achieve first results and the people from our partner organizations were very helpful, as they promised, performing their part in a timely manner and at a professional level.

Project number five. I would like to see myself as a diligent individual and while working on the already existing assignments I tried to find smarter ways to improve and be better at my job. As I mentioned previously you have to be ready for any unexpected situation. You play for the team and you are a team player, so, you have to be prepared to help your associates if needed and at the same time you have to be confident that if you require help yourself your colleagues will do their part too. I was right. Being organized and using the "smarter ways" tactic saved me a lot of time. Once, a few months ago, my Boss, The Goblin, as he does usually, called me in into his headquarters and without any delay asked the following question: "What is more dangerous to an abstract man, a little microbe or a big tiger?"

Not being surprised with the direction into which our conversation went (he is the Boss, he can talk whatever way he pleases) I answered: "Is it some kind of a test?"

Director Goldberg silently took a red colored binder from his working desk and handed it to me saying: "This is a new assignment for you. Take a look. Also, let me explain my question by providing you with an answer. I would like to make sure you understand the importance of the matter and why we take it into our hands."

I decided to go through the file later, after I have all the information, which the director was going to tell me and said: "Please Sir, go ahead. I am ready to listen."

The Goblin continued: "Even the biggest tiger in the world can kill just one or two men maximum; supposedly this animal is really hungry. And a tiny, little microbe can ruthlessly exterminate thousands of people if it is not taken care of. You know the danger of lethal bacteria and how quickly it can spread out."

Being cautious I answered: "Yes Sir, I know."

The director kept going: "Pharmaceutics is a multi billion industry and it takes a lot of time, courage, knowledge, research, money and other resources to produce good medication. And I admire those people who spend years and years working hard, sacrificing their lives for the sake of others. But not everyone is that brave and honest. There are still some cowards who are using their given knowledge and available resources create deadly viruses, claiming they do it for the name of science. Recently we received the Intel that some "toxic" people from one of the "friendly" countries are trying to sell on the black market something like "live cancer cells" as they call it. This disease spreads out very quickly and goes everywhere: public places or private homes, schools or universities and the way it works is that after a person gets infected, the human body fails to recognize the malignant cells and destroy them and as a result that person dies. What is interesting, these "businessmen" assert having medication to treat and to prevent this cancer from happening; it is a kind of virus – antiviral drug thing wrapped up together. They are aiming at selling "the stuff" as a package deal for a very high price. But nothing is pricier than the life of a human being. This extraordinary medication is received from the saliva of one of the rare animals and is very costly and difficult to produce. Of course it is possible to replace it with the generic (analog) medicine, which is cheaper to manufacture compared to the original remedy and more people can afford it. Anyway, I am sure you see the picture."

Yes, I saw the picture and calmly answered the following: "Please Sir, correct me if I am deviating into the wrong direction here, but the way I look at it is that: we need to find the source or the lab where these scary things were created as well as all the people responsible for the cold-blooded creation, who are trying to make money by producing a possible Global disaster. We have to locate and secure the substance before it is too late. We need to obtain the guidelines for the formula of the antiviral drug, which our scientists undoubtedly could use for several good reasons, not for bad intentions and on top of that we need to make sure that these viruses remain canned. Also, since these men are located in a foreign country, we need to stay discreet and not leave any traces of our involvement into the matter even though we are literary trying to "save the World"."

The Goblin said: "You got it right. I want you to travel to this country, meet with those individuals, who are almost certainly just the middle men. Show an interest in their produce; ask questions about the product and what is also very important make an inquiry about the safety of this thing, especially during the transportation. Pretend you are trying to negotiate the price and do not resist too much to their counter offer. Make an effort to buy us some time, but keep them on the hook by acting secretive and being well-off at the same time. I do not have any doubt that these entrepreneurs will follow you. And we will follow them. In all likelihood they will try to check your background on their level. And we do not know what their level is and what kind of connections they have. We do not know who pulls the strings behind the scene. Is it just big headed scientists and their associates, who feel underpaid or is it a bigger game into which some powerful and nasty players might be involved? Now I want you to go and study the information in the binder, think it through and come back with your plans and ideas..."

We said it, we did it. I went to the specified country, met with the sellers, named our price and bought us some valuable time. I am not going to provide all the details of the operation here, but I must say that this is not as simple as it looks on paper. The whole maneuver to create a trustworthy legend and to connect all the dots takes a lot of time and time is a very important consideration. We had to engage many people in the process, tech support and other resources. But the wheel is rolling now, the machine is running and every day I expect to receive a signal to act. We are ready.

Another assignment I am working on is never-ending. It involves observation and gathering Intelligence, analysis and research, cooperation and prevention, anticipation and action. After I was added to the team of professionals, which specializes on monitoring Arms deals, I decided to attach something extra to my everyday duties and schedule.

I formed a list of specific keywords related to the topic and created a number of email alerts by registering with major search engines, industry journals and other websites. This allowed me to stay on top of the game. All I needed to do is to open my electronic mail every day, when I have free time, and read those emails with new information. Of course we have our own ways and systems to monitor the situation around the world, but this simple approach has broadened our reach.

Some countries, especially the superior powers of the modern world have certain directories, which forbid trade of definite armaments. There are a few reasons for having these munitions lists (MLs). It allows the governments to stay in control of what technologically advanced equipment the manufacturers can sell, to whom and to where. You do not want your enemies to attack you or your good friends with your own, homemade, best scientific solutions. At the same time the trade restrictions create an interest in your products. It is in human nature to try to find the answers to the well protected secrets. And this creates demand. Remember the supply – demand rule? If we impose some restrictions on supply and demand stays the same, then the price will go up. It means higher profit. It's all about money at the end anyway.

My goal, with the help of the analysts, team members and other professionals, is to keep an eye on those controlled inventory registers of the different countries and at the same time try to monitor who sold what and to whom. Some sell weaponry, others – strategic resources and so on. We have to observe the ways the military hardware and the related stuff are being traded. And sometimes those ways are totally illegal and against our interests and sometimes, even if they are legal, they are not in favor of the interests of the peaceful people of the world.

Project number seven. Once, not a long time ago, The Goblin appointed me as a curator to one of our young and promising agents to help that agent to create his own "spy system" or a well working and reliable "circle of informants". In particular, I had to help my coworker with the "setting up the net" part into which, according to the plan, an employee of some foreign mission must be caught. That person of interest works as a communications officer and he has access to certain important information, which presents definite significance for us. The man was under surveillance for a few months already and our "watch team" claims they were able to obtain enough reliable data and it is our turn now to make a move.

That agent's name, to whom I was asked to help, is Richard Caberle. Of course Richard had the appropriate training previously and knows what to do, but one thing is to know "the stuff" theoretically and the other thing is to use it in practice. The director decided that I am the best candidate to assist my colleague because I had some prior experience in that area and moreover, I have the necessary teaching skills. Oh, well, no need to admit it, the director is right: I am nice and a very modest person and am really good at what I do.

Anyway, we agreed with Richard to start our work with him by using the combination of theory and practice. First, I asked the man about his view of the ideal spy system in his interpretation. Richard's answer was quite complete, but it seemed to me that he just memorized the school book and his response was not sufficient for me. We had to go through the basics again: a situation could change instantly and an agent must be ready and be able to adjust to it and to act quickly and sometimes this requires breaking "the school rules". Eventually, we came to a conclusion that the system should be simple and independent, secure and reliable, functional and incredibly effective.

The initial contact with the communications officer was successful. Preparation played its part. And of course the surveillance team deserves a special thank you too. Later there were a few more meetings with that officer to establish the ways of communication, information exchange and money transfers. The money question is very important. Even though some individuals naturally need to be involved in something, either because of their character or moral or political beliefs and are ready to work just for the "idea", we need to find the ways to pay them fair amounts of money for the job well done. Throughout some period of time during our work with Richard we visited a few various international conferences. Usually many people attend events like that and it is not difficult to blend in, if you do your homework properly. We targeted a couple of perspective scientists, who are involved in the research and development field. With each following assignment Richard was gaining more confidence – practice makes you better. Also, we had to cover the grounds of some universities domestically and abroad, looking for the right students. If you help young people at an early stage in their lives, then later you will have good assets holding higher positions in the sectors of your interest. Today Richard is a more mature person, a valuable professional, working on his own, but my door is always open for him and I am still involved in his matters and development. We meet periodically to discuss issues and to locate better ways to resolve them. And from time to time

I find myself occupied with Richard assisting him with his ideal "spy system".

And yet another assignment I am working on, this would be project number eight, grasps the very wide area of the use of the Internet's resources. I am not complaining, just emphasizing the fact that in our line of duty you have to be ready to carry a heavy load. Tasks are coming in one by one. You have to be flexible, quick and dependable. These days everyone knows what the Internet is and how to employ it. Some people read the news and play games; others watch movies and so on. The possibilities of the Internet are endless and it is very handy to have the service around.

Once, in recent times, director Goldberg in his usual way invited me to his headquarters. When I entered the director's office The Goblin was looking at the computer screen, watching some Internet video. After the brief greeting the director said: "I suspect they do it on purpose or they are very stupid. But we know for sure that these people are not stupid. They had the proper training and went through a number of tests and assessments. Then it means they have a reason for their actions."

I was just standing there and listening, trying to understand what director Goldberg was saying. Seeing my confusion The Goblin explained: "In the past while, there has been a certain unexplainable tendency in the behavior of our country's servicemen abroad, especially in some hot spots or high risk areas, to be exact. I believe these persons did not want to stay in those countries for their mission, because it is very dangerous. So, they did something stupid and uploaded videos of their horrific actions on public websites, making it available for the view across the whole world and as a result it was a chain of international scandals.

Later these people were sent back to their home country, very alive by the way and not killed in action. Basically they escaped safely from the place in which they did not want to stay. But the question is; before you signed up for the mission, you knew it was going to be dangerous. Why would you agree to something like that and then jeopardize the whole operation and in addition to it produce a bad image of your country?"

I answered: "I heard something about it, but did not see the videos. I am sure there will be fair investigations of these cases. We do not know what happened in reality there, maybe these individuals just tried to attract some attention to a problem, for which they did not see any other way to fix it otherwise?" I cautiously tried to defend those people who were unknown to me, but The Goblin said: "This is not the subject matter I wanted to talk to you about. I would like to ask you to help our "big headed" boys and girls to discover the safe ways of communication for amateurs. We have a lot of "stool pigeons" in different parts of the world, who work for us and we need them and their services. These people provide us with valuable Intel, but for a number of reasons we cannot supply all of them with the means of secure communication. Those undercover agents or informants have to use public computers and the Internet. They have to act average and be average; they have to be unnoticeable and invisible if you will. The reason I asked you to help is that: as opposed to our "big headed" coworkers you are just an average person and you are trained to act and think that way when necessary. You can find simple answers even in the most complicated situations and then "the smart" ones will do their part. You can be some kind of a focus group for them. You will provide our tech staff with the foundation upon which they can build more advanced and secure solutions. This is a long time consuming assignment because the circumstances change constantly and you have to monitor the situation and be able to see the change and adjust to it. Also, you will be travelling sometimes to see for yourself the conditions in which our people work. But I do not think this is going to be a problem for you – you travel periodically anyway."

Even though The Goblin mentioned my "average" mind capabilities in comparison to my other smarter coworkers, the "big headed" boys and girls, I was not angry or upset with him. I knew he was not trying to hurt me or be mean to me. On the opposite, I took the director's statement as a compliment and said: "I understand what is required from me Sir and will do my best as usual."

THE TRAGEDY

That day, as we agreed with Kristina, we were going to visit Romeo at the hospital. We had all the paperwork ready and all the young man had to do was just to sign those papers. And of course before leaving our place of work we first called the unit where Romeo was getting his treatment. The nurse on duty or whoever else it was explained that our patient received another day pass and was supposed to be back around eight o'clock in the evening. This was good news, it means the kid is really getting better if they let him out of the facility that often. So, we rescheduled our visit to the hospital, going there the same day in the evening, instead of at lunch time, hoping that the visitor hours are not over and the hospice workers will allow us to see the patient. Kristina suggested calling the unit again, just in case, to make sure that Romeo is there.

This was one of those rare days for me in the office, when many of my associates were not around. Everyone was somewhere else performing their intelligence work, analyzing something, helping other team members and so on. Some went out to eat or to talk or to carry out different job related duties. It was very quiet in the building and I even thought "why is that?" Suddenly the phone on my desk rang. It was director Goldberg. He asked me to find Kristina and come to see him right away together with her. When we entered the director's study, The Goblin said: "Please take a sit." He looked very upset and sad. After we landed on the chairs by the table, the director continued: "I have horrifying news for you. Just a moment ago Romeo's father informed me that the kid committed suicide. He jumped from a high rise building somewhere in the downtown area." Even though I only knew the young man for a short period of time, I felt like someone poured a big barrel of very cold water on my head. I was shocked and confused with that heartbreaking news. Kristina looked better than I, but I knew somewhere inside her heart she felt the same. We were silent for a moment, trying to realize what had just happened. Probably director Goldberg was able to take control over his emotions quicker than us because he kept going, releasing more details that were known to him. The Goblin said: "The special Police division, which deals with that type of case notified Romeo's family about the accident. They came to the kid's mother's house in person and told her about what had happened, trying to calm the woman down. As you know the Police units have grieving counselors and they offered their services to Romeo's mother, but she refused to accept the moral support. Probably it is very difficult for any human being to think clearly in such situations, but the law enforcement and social services people will keep an eye on her during some period of time. Later Romeo's sister Ena called her father with the sickening news and the distressed man told me on the phone about the calamity."

Kristina and I were soundless, probably thinking the same: "Why? How? Life is not fair. He is too young to die. What went wrong? And so on." In the meanwhile director Goldberg continued: "Right now I do not have any additional information to tell you. My conversation with the kid's father was short and he could not say much anyway."

After this last phrase the director looked at both Kristina and I like he was wordlessly asking if we have any questions. Eventually Kristina said: "Do you know, Sir, when and where the funeral will be held? I think we should go and pay our respect to Romeo and his family. He was a very nice young man." Director Goldberg replied: "I do not know any details yet. Usually it takes a few days to make all the necessary arrangements. I have to find out. According to his father the kid became very spiritual lately and we need to take the religious burial traditions into consideration too. I will let you know as soon as any information comes in."

The rest of the day I spent working on my other assignments and I had to force myself to stay focused. Periodically my memory was bringing up the images of the young man, named Romeo, whom I happened to know for a very short period of time. Later, just before leaving work, Kristina came to talk to me briefly. She said: "I really feel sorry for Romeo's family. Such a loss. He was a great guy, full of life and very kind. Do you think he left a suicide note? Suicides usually leave notes..."

I answered: "I do not know. The director did not mention anything. I am thinking about something else. I remember when the last time we talked with Romeo, he was fine and even promised to start working out again as soon as he got better. And today's news... Life is strange. What went wrong? Were we late? If we just could have met the young man earlier, maybe this would not have happened?"

Kristina was silent for a moment, thinking about something known only to her, then made a statement: "We cannot blame ourselves in this situation. We did everything we could. Of course there are a lot of questions to which I would like to receive answers, but otherwise there is not much we could do. Death is the other side of existence. They go together hand in hand. It's just that you better understand after something like this that life is short and we should take good care of our loved ones and ourselves..."

For the next while we worked in and out of the office, doing regular stuff. Our job is very important and requires a lot of effort, skills, knowledge, concentration and so on. One of those busy days director Goldberg informed me that the memorial service agenda for Romeo was approved by all the parties involved. The Police people have finished their investigation, the medical examiners did their part too, the funeral home was chosen, religious beliefs of the young man were also taken into consideration and so on. The director mentioned that Romeo's father was very grateful to all those folks who helped the family with all the preparations. Also, The Goblin suggested that if we, together with Kristina, want to attend the interment, then we should plan our work beforehand in order to give ourselves an opportunity to pay our respects and say the last "Good bye" to the young man.

On the specified day, when Kristina and I, dressed according to protocol, arrived at the funeral home, there were already a few people in the building: family of the deceased, friends, coworkers of the kid's parents and some other individuals, who happened to know Romeo. I got the impression that everyone loved the guy. He was very kind and honest and respectful. It was really difficult for me to see the sufferings of Romeo's family, especially the father. The man was literary crying. More people, including The Goblin, arrived later. It was a pretty big procession when we headed off towards the cemetery, where everything was already prepared for the final ceremony and burial. Romeo was buried in accordance with the religious tradition and his own values. After the ritual was finished, no one wanted to leave. People were just silently standing there, by the grave, praying for the young man's soul. In due course of the service, someone in the hurry, who kept apologizing modestly, left the place. Then it was another individual and so on. Director Goldberg left too; he is a very busy professional and has an agency to run. The director's attendance of the event just proved his good personality and value of friendship. I even thought that we are very lucky to have him as a Boss. At the end only a small group of people, mostly Romeo's family and best friends, found themselves standing close to each other and talking about their son, grandson and buddy. Eventually, when everyone left the cemetery and only the kid's family members stayed longer, Romeo's father turned to Kristina and me and said: "Thank you for coming. I appreciate it. How did you know my son?"

We introduced ourselves as Mr. Chic and Ms. Jones, Social Workers. Then I explained that we had a chance to meet with the young man earlier, when he was at the hospital, healing his wounds. Ena, Romeo's sister, was standing nearby. Seeing us talking to her father she said: "Hi Mr. Chicken. How are you?" I thought no man on earth wants to be called "chicken", but probably this young lady has a right to call me that. I felt like I could have done more for her brother while he was still alive. Then Ena, addressing to Kristina added: "Hi Ms. Jones."

Both Kristina and I greeted the girl politely. Ena's father with a look of surprise on his face commented: "So, you darling, know these people too?" The girl shook her head like saying "yes", agreeing with her father's question /

statement. Kristina, as a good psychologist, decided to take the initiative into her hands and speaking to the kid's father said: "Excuse me Sir; I know this is a very difficult moment for you and for your family, but is there any place where we could talk about your son?"

The man thought for a brief second, then replied: "We are going to my kids mother's house right now. There is some food that had been prepared. I am sure we can find a quiet room there to chat." When everyone left the cemetery driving their cars, Kristina and I followed Romeo's father in my Mercedes. Kristina said: "I asked the gentleman for a conversation on purpose because I see him suffering a lot and if he has a chance to talk to someone, then he might let go and feel a bit better. Even the toughest men need support sometimes." I just answered: "I see. And thank you for your help."

At the house, when everyone was busy with the food, Kristina, Ena, Romeo's father and I went to the basement area, where there were a couple of couches and a few chairs to sit on, and got engaged in the conversation. Kristina, addressing to Ena and her father, said: "I am really sorry for your loss. Romeo was a very nice young man, incredibly polite and sincere. I liked him a lot. Is there anything we can do for you?" The father replied: "Yes, it is a very tough time for us, but we are okay. Thank you." This time Kristina addressed to Ena only, saying: "You knew your brother better than anyone else. What was he like without that entire defensive attitude young people demonstrate when they are in public, especially around their friends?"

Ena quickly looked at her father, like seeking approval from him to speak, then said: "My brother was and he is still the best to me: very kind and loveable, idealistic and funny, strong and caring. Even in his last message Romeo wrote that he is sacrificing his life for the sake of his little sister. Somehow he believed that she is in danger and the only way to save her is to give up his own life in exchange." Kristina, with a tone of surprise in her voice, reacted: "Interesting... May I please see this note, the last one, which your brother wrote before leaving this world?" Ena again glimpsed at her father, but the man did not show any emotions, thinking probably about his son and the structure of the universe. It was like the "go ahead" signal for Ena and she pulled out a piece of paper from her pocket, with something written on it. "Here, this is a copy, please have a look," said Ena and handed the paper to my partner. Both Kristina and I, with full attention, started reading the message. Yes, it was the suicide note. In the note Romeo mentioned God and God's love to all of us, human beings. He asked for forgiveness, and also begged his family to try to understand him and his deed. Also, Romeo mentioned the little girl, his sister and expressed confidence that now she will be fine. I got the impression, just looking at the young man's writing, that he was very depressed. The lines in the note were sliding downward from left to right. Also, I decided to ask Kristina, the professional psychologist, for her opinion about the message and her view of the content in it, when we have a chance to talk one on one. It is always better to have a second opinion, especially from a qualified person.

When we finished reading the note, Kristina returned the paper to Ena with the following words: "I almost cried reading it. The message is very strong and heartbreaking at the same time. In such a short note your brother was able to show his love for God and to his family, all of you. Also, he talks about the little girl, whom he tried to save. You can tell a lot about his personality from this letter."

At this very moment, looking at Ena, I thought that something is bothering her. The young lady appeared to be depressed, which is totally understandable, and at the same time considerate. Eventually, probably her honest and truth seeking personality won over her hesitation, the youngster being self-effacing said: "May I tell you my true opinion about all of this?"

I was intrigued. It is always interesting to hear the point of view of young people. They are innocent, true and bold. Kristina simply and with encouragement in her voice replied: "Oh, please Ena, go ahead. We will be delighted to listen to what you have to say. You knew your brother better than anyone else; you spent a lot of time with him and obviously have the right to talk."

The girl, still being shy and carefully choosing words, started her speech.

Ena's version.

"Romeo did not die in that accident. It was some staged performance; they, these unknown and dangerous people engaged him in some secret activities. Probably these individuals want to make my brother a Super Spy."

The opening line of this young lady was unexpected to me. Both Kristina and I looked at each other in surprise. Seeing our shocked reactions Ena continued: "Yes, that is what I think. My brother was smart and he still is. And he is strong and the best fighter. He is like a gem stone for those people. And moreover, they, these secret agents or whoever else they are, could easily trick everyone with that incident. Let me explain. I saw that building. The very next day after the "jump" we went there with my father to see for ourselves the place where this terrible catastrophe had happened. You can enter into this residential structure on one side of the building, through the main entrance, which is exactly what my brother did, as they claim, then go straight through the vestibule and exit on the other side of the residence, where a car or a van, parked really close to the back door, is waiting for you. No one would be able to see your maneuver because there are a number of trees in the area, as well as garbage bins."

I think I started getting the idea behind the speech of that clever girl. The more Ena told us, the better we could understand her flow of thoughts. I quickly glimpsed at Kristina. My partner was looking at Ena with an open interest, probably seeing herself at that age. In the meanwhile Ena continued: "I think these secret and scary people took a body of some person who was already dead, and since we live in a big city, a lot of people die every day, then they dressed that dead someone in my brother's clothes and took that lifeless body on the roof. This is a high rise building and you cannot see from the ground if someone, who is standing at the edge of the roof and is ready to jump, is alive or not. I suppose it is possible under these circumstances to hold a dead body in a certain way that the people on the ground, who happen to witness the event, would get a false impression that this person is alive and is going to jump. And even if someone later will question the actions of those surreptitious agents, they can always say in their defense that they were just trying to save the young man's life by holding that young individual by his arms and trying to talk him out of it."

Both Kristina and I were listening to every single word said by Ena. The little girl talked with such confidence and passion that I got the impression that she really believes

173

in her theory. Ena's father was silent and appeared to be thoughtful. Probably they had this talk earlier with his bright daughter. Kristina looked considerate too. Ena continued: "After everything was prepared, all these horrifying people had to do was just let that dead body go, and they had witnesses in the area already, waiting for the event. And moreover, when I was there the next day, at that place with my father; it looked like one "witness" waited for us in the neighborhood to tell his story. Initially that bystander was circling around, like trying to make sure we are the people he saw on some photos shown to him earlier and then later, after the man positively identified us, he made a move. The "eyewitness" declared that he did not see the actual jump, but he saw my brother sitting in the lobby of that building some time prior to the accident. The man said that Romeo appeared to be very sad and depressed. Also, he mentioned that he remembers seeing my brother in the area a few times before and even recalled one case when the Police Officers were called in to remove Romeo from the property. It all looks suspicious to me."

When Ena stopped for a moment to get her thoughts together, Kristina asked the young lady the following: "Tell me Ena, why does it all look suspicious to you?"

The girl replied: "Because the whole chain of events is unreal. I understand, this is life and anything can happen, but in my brother's case the majority of occurrences, which had happened to him, look doubtful and very well orchestrated. We all watch movies and we know there are some bad people out there, who are trying to fix their problems at the expense of others. My brother is alive... When the Police came to my mom's house to tell her about the incident, I was there too. I asked the Law Enforcement Officer right away how they knew that it was Romeo. The policeman answered that they found some identification papers on the dead body, but otherwise the deceased someone was not recognizable at all, after such a long fall. And as I mentioned already, they, these dangerous people, put some dead person into my brother's clothes and the ID's were in the pockets of his attire. Next, after I realized that the Officer I talked to was not convincing enough, I decided to call the medical doctor, who was supposed to do an autopsy on the "jumper's" body."

The intelligent girl stopped talking for a moment, checking our reactions to her words. All of us, including Ena's father, were listening with serious faces and full concentration. You have to be able to pay attention to the opinion of other people, even if they are much younger than you are, if you want to find out something new for yourself or receive more valuable information. Also, I noticed that Ena carefully avoided relating the dead body to Romeo. This was a clear sign that she actually believes her brother is alive or just denies the reality. I decided to ask Kristina later about that.

For the time being the young lady continued: "It was not difficult to find the phone number of the person in charge of the medical investigation. After I called the doctor, the true professional said he did not do anything with the dead body, because the cause of death (COD) was too obvious. Can you believe this? No autopsy or any other examination was done. No checking the chemical components in the brain and body, no blood tests, nothing at all. I think that was a mistake on their part. I am talking about those terrifying individuals, who planned the whole thing. But my question is: are they not, those lab folks, supposed to check the content of the stomach, what was in the blood and so on? Also, no one of us, relatives or friends, saw the body, because it is easy to identify if it was my brother or not. For example Romeo had those knife stabbing wounds on his chest."

After this last phrase said by Ena both Kristina and I meaningfully looked at each other. We noticed from the beginning of the funeral ceremony that the coffin was closed. Closed completely. You cannot see who or what was inside of it. My initial feeling told me that the officials did not want to hurt the family of the young man even more. It is obvious that the loved ones of the deceased had suffered a lot already.

Ena continued: "My brother is a good fighter, the best, and he speaks a couple of foreign languages. I am sure Romeo is alive and probably at this very moment he is going through a far-reaching training at some secret place to become a Super Spy now. Then, most likely, they, these cruel people, will send him to one of those unstable regions, where his new religion is in widespread use, with some hush-hush mission. I might be young, but I pay attention and have noticed that those people in power always use religion to create and escalate conflicts in different parts of the world, because religion for them is the most convenient form of all to justify their actions..."

For the second time, after listening to Ena's words I thought that she is very bright and much more intelligent than the majority of young individuals of the same age. What is more, I decided to talk to director Goldberg about Romeo's sister to help this quick and sharp girl with her personal development and possibly with her future career. Also, even though there could be a number of explanations as to why no one saw the body, why the family did not get any answers to their questions and so on, Ena's deductive reasoning seemed to be delivered in a timely manner and to the point. Anyway, the young lady continued: "I remember myself watching a couple of movies with similar cases. In one movie, I think it was about some Naval Investigative Service, one person was dropped from an airplane, which flies much higher than the height of an average high rise building and still the investigators were able to identify the dead man. The other movie was about a paratrooper, who died because someone deliberately damaged his parachute. And the result was the same. That person was identified too..."

WHAT IF SHE IS RIGHT?

When the tired and emotionally exhausted girl finally stopped bringing out the arguments she had, Kristina politely declared: "Thank you for sharing your point of view with us Ena. It is obvious to me that you love your brother very much."

Romeo's father, after being quiet all this time during his daughter's speech, suddenly decided to start talking. The man said: "This horrifying incident is all shocking and strange to me. My son was not suicidal at all, on the opposite, he was afraid of death. And suddenly he wants to kill himself? I do not believe this. Something had happened, something we do not know… For us he is alive and always will be…"

I sensed a lot of soreness and confusion in that man's words. It is even more painful if you keep all your worries to yourself. And that gentleman is not much of a talker. Kristina, being a professional psychologist, probably saw this "better stay noiseless" character trait in him earlier than me, because she stepped forward saying: "Sir, do you have any thoughts on your daughter's statement? I find Ena's conspiracy theory a little bit odd, but she has her strong points. And she is very observant."

I knew that type of man Romeo's father is. They would not come to you with all their shed tears and complaints.

They will uphold it to themselves suffering in silence. The best way to make people like that to talk is to ask something directly. And after you engaged them into a conversation, keep listening carefully, show you are interested in what they have to say and continue with questions, but do not push it too much.

Romeo's father thought for a moment what to say in response to Kristina's question, then, almost crying, whispered in a low tone voice: "I do not know what to answer. I have so much in my head right now. On one side I understand what had happen to my son, on the other side... What if my daughter is right? And I want to believe she is right. But I have to be realistic and reasonable at the same time. Let's look at the known facts. We did not see the body because the Police folks deal with such cases all the time and they know how agonizing and hard it is for the victims' families to see their loved ones suddenly passed away, especially at that young age. They, the Police, just tried to make it easier for us to go through the difficult times. And I totally understand this. What I do not understand is the behavior of my son for the past while. After Romeo got out of jail, the last time, he gave the impression of being mentally unstable. Something we do not know had happened to him at the detention center. All of a sudden the young man started seeing Angels and the other world. People thought him "crazy", but in reality he saw more than us, so called "normal" individuals. Romeo started believing that he talks to God directly and God asked my son to prove his love for Him... I am not sure if all of this was the result of the use of some psychotropic substances or was it something else. Maybe those hallucinations were side effects of a possible well hidden hypnosis intrusion in combination with dangerous psycho drugs. Or maybe even those mental pictures, we can label them implanted false visions and ideals, were intentionally entrenched into my son's brain for some other purpose? We do not know. Following his release from custody Romeo went through a number of medical assessments and he even applied for the disability support program. And this is a lot of money taken from the government over the years…"

When the man mentioned the "money" question Kristina said: "As I understood, Sir, talking to your son earlier, he was just suffering from post traumatic stress, which is often treatable…"

I am not sure if my partner was trying to divert the man from the "money" topic with that statement or was she just trying to make him talk more by stepping on his sore callus. Because the more the gentleman says, the easier it will be for him to go through the difficult time. And Kristina's trick worked. Romeo's father, with a shaking tone in his voice, replied: "To be honest, I do not have any explanations to the events, which happened to my son and to my family for the past while. And believe me, there were a huge number of occurrences, which should not have happened at all. It was like someone, by the way not God, but a human being, decided to make our life miserable. I got the impression that the majority of events were very well planned and executed."

Then the man glanced directly at Kristina and continued: "If you think I am paranoid, well, I am not. But life is life. And we have to deal with happenings. And every day and every moment of my life I did the best I could to protect the people I love. And now you know I failed, I failed miserably. I brought the best I had here — my family.

I wanted my kids to have a happy life. Today I see it was a mistake; I ruined my family and I could not save my son. It is a punishment for coming here, for the wrong done. I never felt that hopeless in my life than for the past few years. When you experience enormous sufferings day after day, you can easily lose faith in good. But I still believe in God, I still believe things happen for a reason and I hope for the best. I have no one to blame in this situation, but myself. Everyone around talks about a second chance and I never had even the first one. I am not complaining, just trying to find answers to the questions I have. And I have the whole bunch of them. Questions to doctors, to probation officers, to different counselors, to correctional officers and so on. The system failed my son, the system failed us."

Listening to Romeo's father I thought that the man is very emotional and probably has a lot to say. I think I even saw some tears in his eyes. When life is tough on you, ordinary things look very different, compared to the time when everything was right and you and your loved ones were happy. Kristina, with a sympathetic face, kept on being silent, periodically nodding her head, like she was encouraging the gentleman to say more. Ena appeared to be surprised a little bit as well. She had probably never seen her father in such an expressive condition. In the meanwhile the man continued: "In fact, I have a feeling that the kid knew that the system failed him. And I even believe, somewhere inside my heart, that my son's often inappropriate behavior was, in a certain manner, his way of protesting. Romeo most likely wanted to prove to those big boys and big girls that he does not need their false words and actions. I accept it as true that he tried to show the world that he could distinguish himself from right and wrong. Yes, Romeo had some problems with the law, but he wanted to change. My son could see when people, especially the so called "successful individuals", would tell lies…"

Then Romeo's father stopped talking for a brief second, looked at Kristina and me like he was trying to prevent the potentially forthcoming argument, and continued: "I know what you may think, but no. No, it was not jealousy, if you will. Romeo was not envious at all. It is just that he could not accept the dishonesty and the false statements of some cunning people when he clearly saw the opposite in their actions. You have to practice what you preach. Somehow my son understood the structure of this world differently than the majority of the general public does. We are all unique, but not every one of us has the ability to recognize the true purpose of life – that is our Spiritual Growth. In reality the kid perceived a greater number of fundamental signs from that undiscovered side of the universe, which we are all eagerly wondering about, than us "normal" people. He also recognized that there is a purer sustenance to life, which is much more spiritual than in the ways this world offers it to those people who do not bother to learn about it. When my memory periodically brings up the unusual content of the conversations we had with my son, before his departure from this world full of sins, I tend to believe to a greater extent that Romeo was able to look into a different dimension. He told me that he saw the other world, where all individuals are friendly and equal. They do not eat each other like wild animals do, but on the opposite – they help one another. He saw a diverse world, the world we can only dream of. A world without wars, a world without betrayal, a world where kindness and compassion, sympathy and care, respect and honor are not just words, but underlie the way of life."

All this time, while we were having that conversation, Romeo's father was speaking with exceptionally touching energy. He spoke with a low tone and almost without any facial or bodily expression. The man was solid like a rock and at the same time appeared to be in severe emotional pain. His daughter Ena, after her daddy took a small break to get his thoughts together, stepped forward saying: "My brother changed significantly in the past while. And he changed for the better. Let me give you just one example of his new behavior. Once, not long ago, we went to the park with Romeo that is in his neighborhood, close to his residence, to get some sun, talk about life and spend time together. When we were at the park, we saw a lot of parents with their kids playing and enjoying themselves. At the same time there was a lot of garbage on the ground. My brother started cleaning the area. He picked up every single piece of waste and threw it in the trash bin. I helped him too. Romeo said that children deserve healthier conditions to play their games in. Of course you know kids, it is in their nature to touch something dirty and then put their fingers into their mouth and this is very dangerous for their wellbeing."

When the young lady finished her story, Kristina said: "You are right Ena, I also noticed that your brother was very kind and strong. It takes courage to do something like that, which you just told us about."

Probably the kid's father, in spite of everything that was already told here, still had a lot on his mind to share because the gentleman said: "Time after time I keep asking myself the same question: what if my daughter is right?"

Seeing the looks of puzzlement on Kristina's and my face, the man explained: "I am talking about Ena's theory. What if my son is alive and was drafted by some Intelligence

Agency or a third party? It means they, these secretive folks, are going to train and use him and other young people like him who were taken away from their families without their parent's consent. I do not know if you are familiar with the latest events in our city, but let me just provide you with more information on that. According to one of the local TV news stations there has been a chain of deaths of young people in the town during the past few weeks. These young men and women were about the same age as my son. And all those deaths had happened throughout a short period of time, a few weeks to be exact. This is very suspicious. Apart from others, there have been a number of deaths in just one local neighborhood. Six young men, belonging to the same community, died in different accidents. And those were immigrants or the children of immigrants who came here to find a better life and they came into this country from the same fatherland. And as you have figured out already, that country is located in some unstable region, on a distant continent. When I heard the news, then I saw the pattern. To me it looked like it was some kind of a recruitment process for some secret and very powerful organization. One may say that I am wrong, that it was just a coincidence. And I would agree. Most likely it is. But I am a father and if I see even the slightest, tiny chance that my son is alive, I will take it. Also, as I was told by some smart people, coincidence requires a lot of preparation..."

Listening to the distressed man I thought that he must really be in pain to make statements like that and to see conspiracy everywhere. Kristina probably thought the same because with a look of surprise on her face she said: "It is an interesting hypothesis Sir. But why would some powerful organizations, as you claim, go through such a complicated process to hire new people? As I understand these institutions have their recruiting ways, meaning they usually check the background of their prospective candidates and typically call to verify the applicant's references. Also, they, the recruiters, very often put those potential employees through a number of different tests and assessments, but I do not think they do something severe as officially killing, even on paper, their future staff members."

Ena's father replied in frustration: "Because they are dominant and smart and because these scary people think way ahead. And also, I believe, because they can get away with all of that. With just one "simple move" these folks saved themselves a lot of headache and money. Let me explain. After the right candidates have been chosen, then the schooling for them should begin. And after the training of the new contenders they, these powerful organizations, will send those young workers to some unstable regions or back to their native countries. And usually it is with a mission to make those countries even more unbalanced or to organize revolutions and to change unwanted governments. What if something terrible happens to these new members of those secret associations after they have arrived to their final destination? Then there is a huge possibility that a lot of "Why?" questions will arise. And next, the conspirators will have to answer the tough questions which may come from the families of the victims, their friends and lawyers. And by the way, as everyone knows, those representatives of law are frequently eager to get noticed and earn themselves some publicity as well as some extra cash. Often in such circumstances families will inquire if their kid had proper training and usually seek compensation, which could potentially be measured as tons of money, or expressed in millions of dollars. And I am not even mentioning the possibilities of various political scandals. But here is the catch: if the kid is already dead to his or her family members and to everyone else, then you see for yourselves: there aren't any traces, which could lead to the initial planners, left behind. And if there are no traces, then it means no cases..."

The man stopped for a moment, inhaled some air and continued: "What if all of this is true? Hypothetically speaking? I am just saying. Then it is very scary, very inhuman like and very dangerous. It is risky to the whole world, especially to the people in those poor regions as well as to these young individuals themselves. Again, if my daughter's assumption is correct and these new recruits do exist, then it means they are zombies, because they were brainwashed and made humanlike robots. And these fresh hires will do whatever they are told to do without asking any questions. Officially they are dead and have nothing to lose or to be scared of. Almost certainly the organizers, those merciless people who are in charge of all the conspiracy, showed the newly selected recruits the videos of their own funerals with the tears of their parents, family members and friends. And of course they gave them new passports with new names. It is all really possible in theory and if it is possible in theory then it is even more possible in practice. And this is very frightening and not right. If your own government is letting you down, the possibility of such a program is real, then I am sure someone would know that this type of plan does exist. Shame on them if this is all true. And if this is the case, then what future does this country have? I am sure there is God. And God will step in to make things right, when the time comes... No matter what, but in the last part of any affair each person will receive not what he or she wishes, but what they actually deserve… At the end, Good will always win over Evil…"

Looking at Romeo's and Ena's father I almost cried myself. The gentleman was in real pain. I thought that he needs help from a professional psychologist or a similar professional to deal with his emotional problems. It was obvious to me that the man had that type of a mental breakdown, when his rich imagination flew far above the ground. I even thought that he could easily become a fantasy writer, having thoughts like that. But on the other hand you have to understand the guy. He just lost his son. Perhaps it is the end of the world for him. Kristina, who knows much more than I do in the mental problems field, with a very calm voice said the following: "Sir, I am not going to argue with your proclamations, evidently you have your strong points. It is just that I think those doctors, who had a chance to treat your son, would disagree with you."

I think my partner provoked the man on purpose with these words. She wanted him to express his anger and nuisance. She wanted him to let it go for his own good. And it worked. Ena's father said: "My ex wife has a couple of friends, who are medical doctors by the way. Ena showed the prescription for my son to those doctors and both of them claimed that the medicine prescribed was just the regular sleeping pills. Also, both men said it in such a way that it was obvious to me that they questioned the chosen method of treatment. But I think otherwise. I suspect those doctors, whoever they are, and who prescribed the sleeping pills to my son, are part of the same scheme as those secret people who pulls the strings behind the scene. You know it is like in sports. Some doctors supply steroids to certain athletes to make those sportsmen stronger and faster. Even if they know it is completely illegal, they still do it. Same here. If I am right, then these doctors play for the same team as those conspiracy men and these people are geniuses. You cannot link those doctors to the brainwashing process. When the kid was inside the therapeutic facility, he was getting one type of meds, which we can call psychotropic and probably underwent hypnosis sessions. When they let him out, they officially gave him the sleeping pills to cover their traces. Now, if the family or friends of the deceased decide to take those doctors to the court of law, to answer for their actions, the doctors are clear. They can always explain that the diagnosis was just post traumatic stress and that the patient needed some rest and that is why they prescribed those resting pills. Nothing fancy or against the law."

Again, when the man stopped for a moment to catch his breath and to get his thoughts together to better explain the conspiracy theory, Kristina politely made a remark: "Very interesting, Sir, very interesting." She said this phrase in such a way, that it was obvious to me that she is encouraging the gentleman to talk more. And Romeo's father continued: "If this is all true, then it is very scary... And it means these people, doctors and others, do it often. They know what to expect and how to cover their footprints and trails."

The daughter of this distressed man, young, smart and beautiful Ena, decided to stop the emotional torment of her father by changing the topic of the conversation. Probably, Ena had noticed the reactions of disbelieve on our faces to the words said by her anxious father. So, the girl decided to get in the way and announced the following: "I think the food is ready. We should go upstairs and join everyone else."

Both Kristina and I looked at Ena's father like mentally

asking him if he is done with his story and ready to go. The man realized that everyone is waiting for his decision and said: "My daughter is right. We should go now, but let me just finish the thought I have. Not long ago, approximately a few weeks before this horrific accident, and after Romeo healed his knife wounds, he came to me and asked if we can train together for a while. There is a stadium near the place where I live and the owners of the facility allow average people to just go there and practice for free. It is a very nice gesture on their part. Anyway, let me get back to the story. After my son asked me if I can help him to get back in shape, I was very happy. And of course I quickly agreed to his proposition. This was not anything new or unusual for us. We used to work out together all the time, since my son was a little kid, learning to walk. And I still practice sometimes in the company of my daughter Ena, when I have a chance. At first, Romeo was slow and he could get tired very easy, but later, subsequent to just one week of hard training, he became much better. My son is that type of person whom nature gave a lot: strong, fast and full of life. We trained everyday for about ten days in a row. I tried to make it easier for him by often suggesting to not push himself very hard. It is very important not to overload yourself at the beginning, while your brain and body are not ready yet for the heavy practices. Everything was good and according to the plan. And then, suddenly, Romeo stopped coming to work out. Yes, he still visited me almost every day, but refused to exercise. And he did not provide any explanations for his behavior. I am telling you about this happening, because it looked suspicious to me. I got the feeling that someone told my son to come practice with me for some time, like they, these unknown people were trying to see what shape Romeo is in."

When the man told us this little story, Kristina just pronounced calmly: "Interesting." And that was it. I was quiet. Ena got up from her seat, ready to go upstairs. Her father stood up too, but before going, he made his final statement for that day. Or should I say it was more like a request for forgiveness. The man, still being in a state of agony, said:"You know what? Please forget everything I told you and what my daughter said too. It was pain talking, not me. Also, I want to apologize in front of you for my words and honesty. I do not want you to think that I am crazy."

Later, when Kristina and I left Romeo's mom's residence and were riding in my car, I asked the professional psychologist for her opinion about the suicide note written by the young man and about her view of the content in it. Kristina said: "We cannot take sides in this matter. Yes, the kid's father is upset and he told us a lot of things he should not have... But we are all human beings and sometimes we can be strong and every now and then we can be weak, and that is exactly his condition at the present time. Anyway, it is obvious to me that the note was written by Romeo himself, because his family knows his handwriting and they did not question the authenticity of the letter. I got the impression reading it that the kid was trying to save his little sister by sacrificing his own life in exchange. He believed that God told him to do that. At the same time I know that Romeo previously underwent some type of hypnosis sessions, done by certain unknown and skilled people. If you ask me if it is really possible that these mysterious folks were able to implement false visions and delusions into his head, then my answer would be yes. Unfortunately, we did not have enough time to work with the young man to break through the defense mechanism in his mind."

Even though everything was almost clear to me, I still decided to ask my partner for her opinion about "Ena's version" that Romeo was drafted by some secret agency. And I said: "Kristina, what do you think about the theory given to us by Ena and her father? Is there any chance they might be right?"

Smiling politely the psychologist replied: "I believe everything is possible, especially in our line of work. You tell me, you have more experience..."

A Powerful Prayer

That evening, after Romeo's funeral, I lay down on the sofa in front of the TV set at my place and decided to watch some news. It was a very long day for me and I needed to switch my mental focus onto something different to help divert my thoughts from the sad events of the past day. Some people suggest getting drunk in situations like this. They claim it works. Well, not for me. Of course you can drink as much as you can and then lose your precious consciousness for a while, waking up some time later in your own or someone else's vomit excrements, trying to remember what had happened. I cannot afford that. I have to be sharp and quick all the time, even when my mind and body cries for help, if I do not want to lose my job.

I was probably really tired both mentally and physically that day, because somehow, despite the noise created by the TV set, I quickly fell asleep. In my strange dream I found myself standing at the top of a very high mountain, looking at a very bright source of light. As soon as I saw the world around me from that high spot, something like an electric switch or a similar device, clicked in my head and I suddenly realized that it was God's light. Everything looked so genuine to me at that exact moment that I did not even know what that was: a vision, a simple dream or reality. And then I heard a voice: "Life is a Battle and it is a Battle for everyone; it does not matter if you are rich or poor, strong or weak, healthy or sick. Sometimes you win, sometimes you lose. And when you win you enjoy the victory and you want to win again and again, because the taste of success is sweet. And you are ready to move mountains to get that satisfying feeling once more. And if you lose, you may be destroyed by your malfunction or as I suggest, you better learn from your failure and get stronger. So, when the next fight comes, you will be ready. You will push yourself much harder. And you will try to win. Hard work pays and if you stay honest to yourself and to others, you will eventually win. With those life Battles comes your vital experience: frustration or satisfaction, love or suffering, joy of life or disappointment in life and with this divine knowledge comes your Spiritual Growth. And Your Spiritual Growth is the whole idea of living. When the Holy Light visits you, consider it as a sign that you passed the initial tests and are ready for something bigger. For example: some people become charitable businessmen, others just help those in need and so on. But everyone, who was chosen, is in the process of contributing to the happiness of those still in the darkness and to the wellbeing of the entire Universe."

Then I noticed a big screen in front of me, like I was somewhere in the movie theatre. And on the panel I could see different images. Those were the pictures of people in need: homeless, disabled, mentally challenged, war and hunger victims, ill and poor. At that moment I had a very frightening and unbearable sensation in my mind and body. That agonizing feeling came to me from just looking at those scary illustrations. Next, my imagination in no time took me far away from that high mountain and I found myself walking on the streets of some big city. Being in that place was very emotionally painful for me, especially when I saw one mentally challenged person, standing at the intersection of two streets. The man was physically present there, but probably he was somewhere else in his brain, because the weather was very cold and rainy and that gentleman did not feel any of it. He was standing at the same spot, not moving far away from it and arguing with someone invisible. That picture was very heartbreaking. I walked by that less fortunate person going my way and returned back about one hour later or so, at least that is what I felt like in my dream. And the man was still standing there. Suddenly, I remembered Romeo when I saw him in that same abstract condition as that gentleman on the street was in. For a split second I felt like I do not understand God. And I had so many painful "Why?" questions in my head. It was and it is very hurtful to me to see all these people who struggle and suffer every day of their lives. And I started begging God to help those in need. I think, I even wrote a prayer called "Please God help us and forgive us all" in my sleep. The prayer went like this:

In troubles to the hilt,
Guilty without guilt,
Being a loser and feeling odd
I was addressing directly to God:
"Life is not easy
And the cheese I eat is not cheesy
Being held in thrall
With no help at all
I found my way to You
Without any clue
I think it is awesome
And I want to be a better person

I want to change my life
I want to win that strife
You're probably busy helping others
Our mothers and brothers
And I agree with You
They need help more than I do
But I still need Your blessing
I want to eat food with dressing
I want things changed
And I know it can be arranged
Covered with dust
I was living in my past
I can shake that dust away
And be on my way
To become a new man
I know I can
We can't understand Your game
But You created this World with an aim
For people to live in joy and fame
And I would like to proclaim
The hope is still alive
And I will survive
Because wherever I go
You are with me, I know
Thank You for Your attention,
Inspiration and motivation
Thank You for changing my angle of view
And Thank You for everything You do"
I wrote this powerful prayer
Being in a state of despair
This improved my mood
I did not know I am that good

Then I heard a voice:
"It is your choice
Do not surrender
And always remember
Start and finish your day
With a pray
This is serious,
Not a play
Forget the word whatever
And never say never
Work on your attitude
And always express your gratitude
Do not take things for granted
Protect what was already planted
Do not leave children in a state of neglect
And treat others with respect
These are the simple rules
Use it as powerful tools
Remember it is divine
And you will be doing just fine…"

Sometime later, still being in my dream, I was walking
on the streets of the same city without any purpose that was
known to me. There were a lot of people around and no one
was looking at a perfect stranger or paying attention to my
business. I, on the opposite, saw everything. Somehow my
vision was extreme and I was able to read people's minds and
to see their pain, problems and fears. Moreover, one way or
another, I knew how to help those folks in need. At that time
the voice said again: "Remember, you are not alone. There
are many other individuals just like you. You will find them
when the time is right. Your potential today is a valuable
gift for you. You are capable of seeing more and thinking

deeper than many others can do. Use it for Good. If you don't, in that case this valuable gift will become a severe punishment... Because when you help others, you feel excellent, you feel satisfied and that someone needs you. It is a great sensation. But, on the other hand, if you are gifted and you use your gift for your own sake, by being selfish, rude and causing harm to others, then the punishment is inevitable."

Something barely discernible for the human eye gave me the strength and the courage to open my mouth and with an unusual bravery for me I said: "I know You are very powerful, like anything else or anyone else on this Earth and Your presence here, in this World, is everlasting. I am not going to waste Your sacred time, but I have to ask this, just one, question: Why do we, by we I mean the human populace in general, have to suffer?"

The voice replied: "Not necessarily. It is the choice people made. You are familiar with the term "Joy of Life" and as you know life is the most cherished gift of all. People suffer because it is a way of payment for the sins they committed. There are certain principles that exist, of which you can learn in many ways: through religion, school, from your parents and so on. And if you follow these principles, you will be fine. Life on the Earth's plane of existence is precious and is given to human beings primarily for Spiritual Growth. Remember that, follow the rules and help others."

At that moment I woke up. The TV was still showing the same news program. I automatically looked at my wristwatch, only twenty minutes had passed since the program started. I did not miss much. Being under the impression of my vivid dream and in spite of the unusual and strange contents of this vision I thought it is really amazing how quickly you can travel from place to place in your sleep. Also, I thought that the human brain works in a miraculous way and the capabilities of it are endless. It was time for the Sports news and my attention switched back to watching the TV. Almost certainly I was too tired that day. I do not know how and when, but I fell asleep again. And I fell asleep just about instantly. All I remember is that: I was thinking "What is wrong with me? Maybe I work too much or maybe it is something else?" Then, by some means, my mind returned me back to the reverie I saw a few moments ago. I see dreams all the time, everyone does, and there is nothing wrong with that. But this one, the one I saw just now, is really strange and "wild". I would even call it "meaningful with important effects on my future life". The light I saw and the voice I heard were more than real. And the message delivered was true and powerful: "Life on the Earth's plane of existence is precious and is given to human beings primarily for Spiritual Growth. Remember that, follow the rules and help others."

Then, my mind played another trick on me. This one was job related. I found myself being a diligent student sitting in a classroom. Actually, there were only two students in the whole class: my partner Kristina and I. And the subject we studied was called "Spirits' Intelligence or the use of the Soul for Intelligence Operations". The teacher, somehow I do not remember her name, was one of the strongest Psychics known worldwide. She said to us: "I am sure you know that there are some people out there who are able to talk to Spirits, to the Souls of the people that have passed away. And those Psychics, or individuals with special abilities, as they are sometimes called, are often used by the Police or other law enforcement agencies to help with their investigations and research of something unknown and complicated. This topic we study today is not advertised much and you would not find any specific details about it in the publicly accessible sources. Yes, there is some basic information available here and there, but no particular facts on how it is done or how these people communicate with Spirits. And each one of those Gifted Persons has their own routine, procedure or secret, their own technique to correspond with the outer world and receive data.

Now, let's think about traditional secret agents, the way they infiltrate into different organizations to gather Intelligence and all the other related stuff. Just imagine how risky and difficult it is for them to congregate Intel today, with the employment of all those protective resources against them, such as the use of security cameras and advanced computer programs, tracking devices and hidden microchips. Firstly, it takes time to find and train the right individual. Secondly, it takes time to create a reliable and adequate legend for that mole. Modern safety measures are so advanced, that the Intelligence agent must be able to think on his or her feet and think quickly and not in a commonly established way to beat the defense mechanism in order to get what's required. And if the person on the inside, the infiltrator, gets caught, then the whole operation, including the other people involved, is under a real threat. And with the failure comes the possibility of a political or international scandal.

The discovered link between Psychics and Spirits, on the other hand, gives totally new directions and opportunities. What if, hypothetically speaking, the Psychic and this particular person, who is about to die, meet each other while this dying someone is still alive and establish trust between them. What if, in theory, this leaving this world someone agrees to help with something after their death and becomes the eyes and ears of that Psychic in the other dimension? They set up methods of communication and what data to look for after that person departs from life, because the Psychic already knows how to exchange information with Spirits. After that, when this "Spirit agent" crosses over into a different world, they see no borders, no boundaries, no walls... That Spirit can travel anywhere, and then communicate their findings into this world. Do you get the idea? This will be a breakthrough for any Intelligence Service who is able to discover or develop this "technology". Just think about it again. And by the way, this is my intellectual property..."

At that moment I woke up. And I knew what I have to do next. But before going to The Goblin with that "crazy" idea, I have to first go through a lot of research related to the "interesting topic". We have certain lists or databases, if you will, with information about interesting people. I need to go all the way through those lists; I have to check as many attention grabbing subject matter cases as I can. And of course I have to talk to many different people with suitable experience as well as to verify correlated medical occurrences, which are freely available through public sources. And then, after I have enough reliable and important information, I will again think it through and decide if I should waste the valuable time of my superiors.

Of course you know what usually happens, when you bring forward some new out of the ordinary initiative. Most likely you will be the one responsible for the implementation of it. It is like an unwritten rule of some sort of punishment for the inventiveness. And as I mentioned earlier, I am already very busy. But there must be a serious motive for me seeing that type of dream. And I believe things happen for a reason. It could be a great opportunity as well. You do not want to miss out on great opportunities. I am not talking about personal promotions or the possibilities of earning some extra cash; it is obvious to everyone already. What I am saying is that it could be a breakthrough in the whole system of Intelligence work. It could be the future.

Live Happy

When I showed up at work the next day, I was fresh, sober and ready to go frontward with my usual energy and drive. The past night's evocative and challenging dreams were sitting somewhere in my brain and I decided to spend about fifteen minutes per day on the appropriate research and formation of that new "extreme" idea. The technological aspects of the whole process of bringing into play human Souls as secret agents gave the impression of being within the reach of modern know-how. If they can perform complex heart operations in hospitals and return hopeless and desperate patients back to life or send spaceships to land on other distant planets, then something like I saw in my dream last night comes into view as really achievable.

I spent that morning working on my other projects: reviewing, fixing, analyzing, covering up and discovering new ways and directions to better do my job. During lunch time Kristina suddenly emerged at my desk out of nowhere and invited me to go with her to talk to one university professor, who is the internationally recognized star in a certain field of some intricate studies. Kristina said that the gentleman used to be her college teacher and is very interesting to talk to. She said he knows a lot and always has his own opinion on global events. I was more than glad to have the opportunity to meet with some extraordinary and open minded person, even if it was the dining time for me. And as you know, men do not like skipping their meals... To my unexpected relief, the meeting took place at some student's café on the university grounds, which is located not far from our building, just ten or so minutes away by car. And by the way you can buy pretty decent food there, at that place.

The professor, a man in his early fifties, was dressed like a teenager, wearing a pair of jeans, a pair of running shoes and a brightly colored jacket. Probably the youthful environment played its part for him to choose that type of attire. I am not judging, just saying. I like to dress like a teenager myself. After the initial formal greetings, we bought some provisions and landed at one of the empty tables in the far corner, where not that many students were present. Actually it was a quiet area, well hidden from the general academia public.

Kristina needed to talk to the professor about some stuff, psychosomatic related, and while they were having a conversation, I was eating. What do you expect? I am not that good at analyzing the behavior of different criminals, scammers and other con artists. Most of the time during the conversation Kristina asked specific questions and the professor was answering them. Then my partner would clarify doubtful elements and make notes. At the same time, somehow, both of them managed to eat their food. Probably their student years did not pass by without teaching them at least something: for example how to eat in a hurry. I finished my meal quickly and was just sitting there, slowly sipping the cranberry juice I bought. Seeing a lot of confident, optimistic, full of vigor and smart students around, my memory cogently brought back the pictures from the past when I, myself, was in their shoes. At that age everyone believes that the bright future is in front of them and I think it is good. Because this is true. If you work hard and know exactly what you want, then the result will come. And to be totally honest, I envy in a good and positive way those young people, who have the guts to follow their dreams. Being particularly busy with my thoughts and meal, I was not listening much to what Kristina and professor were talking about, but at some point the word "suicide" pronounced by the professor caught my attention. The gentleman was eagerly stating: "Let me explain it to you in simple words. There are some well-known classifications that exist, such as "suicide" and "self-sacrifice". And they are diametrically opposite in their meaning. Sometimes people refer to those categorizations as "critical points", I am sure you learned that long ago, and if someone reaches these so called "critical points" in their life, then the shift goes inadvertently to the entirely reverse direction: torment and enormous suffering or eternal happy life."

The professor stopped for a split second to drink some milk he chose for himself while ordering his snack and seeing that I am listening too, continued with even more enthusiasm: "The out of the ordinary thing here is that: death is the final result of both these "suicide" and "self-sacrifice" events. At the last part of the episode the person or persons are dead. But what is interesting is the impact, following the death, on the existence of the deceased after their passing, in the afterlife. The outcomes at the end of those events are complete polar opposites. This is because in each case, the passing away of an individual has a totally different sign and meaning. In both cases the death of a physical body is not the death of a Spirit. It is a transition for a Human Soul from this material world into a real death world, such as Hell or a transition into the world where everlasting joyful life exists, such as Paradise. And sometimes this changeover is really scary and painful."

The professor stopped his explanations again to get his thoughts together and, probably noticing my confused reaction to his words, after drinking more milk, continued: "Let me just clarify this: suicide is the act of deliberately killing yourself and the punishment for it is severe. Self-sacrifice, on the other hand, is sacrifice of one's personal interests or well-being for the sake of others or for a good cause and the reward for it is life in Heaven."

Now, I think, I started perceiving the point of view provided by that extraordinary man. I do not know why he was telling us about those atypical things, probably Kristina has asked him something, but what the gentleman said in the last part of his speech was interesting and even I could understand him. In the meantime my partner made a comment: "I really feel sorry for the family of that young man. This is such an enormous loss for them. You give the best to your kids and you want them to be healthy and happy. And I would not wish any parent to see their child die…"

In response to the testimonial made by Kristina the professor whispered: "Once one really smart person said: "When you come into this world as a newborn baby, you cry, but everyone is happy. And when your time comes and you leave this world, you are happy, but everyone is crying…""

I decided it is time for me to show that I am participating in the conversation too and with a provocative and objectionable tone of voice I surreptitiously announced: "Is this not Ironic?" The professor silently looked at me in such a way, that it was obvious to me that he was questioning my intellectual and moral abilities. The gentleman probably saw much worse in his career, teaching others most of his life, because a moment later, after carefully examining my facial features, the man turned his head back to Kristina and continued like I was not even there at all: "You know, my students and I at present are conducting a research study on the effect of nicotine on brain activity of non smoking individuals and particularly on memory and attention aptitude. And the first results we received are quite interesting. I think, if you have the time, you should come and see for yourself."

I automatically noticed that the professor was not ignoring me and he was not rude by any means; it is just his profession and the knowledge of how valuable time could be, played its part. Probably the man, being really busy, appreciated every free minute he had and I, with my sudden comment reminded the university lecturer of some of his sluggish students, who like spending his expensive time irrationally. Anyway, it was the point for me to make a phone call. I had to make a call to a friend of mine, one of our high profile tech specialists. This "Magician", as we call him among us, the other employees of the agency, suggested that I should install a couple of tiny video cameras on my car to record everything around and moreover, the man expressed the willingness to do it himself. You cannot turn down an offer like that. The expert claimed it would not cost much nowadays, with all those advanced technological solutions, but having cameras will certainly help me to spot if someone is showing unnecessary attention to my modest personality. When somebody is after you, especially if it is a team of professional surveillance boys and girls with access to many cars and other modern equipment, it is almost impossible to notice their presence. But having the visible documentation of your daily activities gives you a good chance to recognize the same face seen twice a day or a car, which happened to follow you, even in a certain distance, on a few occasions during a short period of time...

So, I apologized to Kristina and the teaching chief and went outside to make a phone call letting those science belonging people return back to discussing the "interesting stuff", for instance: brain structure and which part of it answers for sleepiness and which part is responsible for bad habits, such as drinking or gambling.

When I called this coworker and friend of mine, who by the way was expecting the phone call from me, the "Wizard" politely recommended that I should come visit them at the end of the operational hours. In this case I would not interrupt with their and my own work. After the telephone chat I decided not to go back to the café and was just standing at the parking lot next to my car, enjoying the weather and the view of the young and bright people around. Sometime later Kristina and the internationally recognized star joined me. Professor, being a gallant and noble man, walked Kristina out of the building and at the same time he wanted to say good bye to me. It was a nice gesture. Also, we exchanged business cards with the genius. Of course my card was simple, only some basic info on it. The professor's calling card was impressive. It had a colorful picture of a human brain on it as well as some fancy words like "great thinker", "cortex", something else, similar in nature, and his contact information. Looking at the professor's card I even thought that the gentleman is not scared to be different. Good for him. He earned it and he earned my respect. When Kristina and I were in the car, driving back to work my partner mentioned that she loves the professor guy and that he is always ready to help his current and former students, if his assistance is needed. Also, Kristina mentioned some complicated process of formation and movement by certain brain neurons, which causes schizophrenia, and that she needed to discuss it with her teacher. She said it was very important for her to better identify something and I am glad I was able to help by driving her to this meeting, even though I myself did not understand a thing they said when they were discussing that topic.

At the end of the day, as we agreed with the "Magician", I went to see him. First the "Wizard", using some high tech equipment, quickly checked my car for unwanted bugs and other tracking devices. We, all employees of the agency, periodically do those "health" checks just to be on the safe side. There are a lot of "strange" people out there who are nosy and would like to know what others are up to. And they are even ready to pay good money for such information. So, the precaution measures are necessary. After the initial part, when the man was satisfied with his security routine, the "Magician", with the help of his partner, the other "Juggler", installed the essential gear on my exquisite car. When the job was very well done, a friend of mine said: "Serge, this is a fine piece of the best technology and allows a real time transmission of the data received. It automatically scans car's plate numbers and red flags anything suspicious. Also, this thing, as you usually say while talking about high tech devices, has face recognition capabilities and a few more features. And of course, you know it already; you have to pay for the equipment through the official channels."

"Okay, I got it, but let me take you and your colleague here for a nice dinner, with beer and everything… Just to show my appreciation for your help. I know a couple of good places," was my response. "Surprisingly" both men quickly agreed to my offer and moreover, we did some kind of a test drive on the way to the eating place, checking the new gear and how it works. Everything was in order and the men explained to me what things to look for to make sure that I get the most of the technology.

There were just a few people at that time of day at the eating place. Somehow we continued our brainstorming session at the same time as enjoying our meal and drinks. The "Magician" said: "Serge, modern technology is what makes us better than others. You have to respect your opposition, whoever they are. And it means that these people from the rival camps have about the same IQs as we have. Of course this would depend on the task at hand and the level of the game, but on average I would rate them to be equal. This means our victories, and as I understood we keep winning, are mostly based on the up to date scientific solutions that we utilize.

Of course no one cancelled the so called "Human Factor" yet. And our people are our pride. Evidently we have the best of the best. But all of our victories would not have happened without the advanced technological tools, which have already been mentioned previously, that we had developed and often had to use in order to beat the competition. Also, these great accomplishments would be impossible without the additional proper steps we take; such as the appropriate process of selecting new employees and the prudent training of our specialists or, for example, the many different possibilities of personal development on the job and the love for our country as other example. And personally, I think that being patriotic is a huge contributor to the overall success of any campaign."

Both listeners, the other "Juggler" and I, quickly agreed with the devoted speech of our good friend. Then we ordered more beer. To be absolutely honest, I barely touched the drinks, because I appointed myself as the designated driver. And I also kept in mind that after we finished here I would have to deliver the "Magicians" to their respective homes, safe and sound. We play for the same team and we have a lot of work in front of us in the near future.

It's Your Pick

In the morning, when I showed up at the workplace, I found a memo at my desk left by director Goldberg. The note said that The Goblin is going on a business trip to some specified location and will be absent for a period of a few days. The director apologized that he could not talk to me personally. As I understood he left the office, and the country, in a hurry. No problem, this way of communication works for me too. And the director acted according to the situation and it is a part of the job to be able to act and react and adjust quickly. Also, The Goblin wanted me to do some important work for him and for the country, if you will, and he left the detailed instructions on how to get it done.

After getting myself familiar with the directives, it took me some time to realize exactly what was required of me and what the overall situation was like. Director Goldberg, being one of the top professionals in our field of work, could see deeper and further than others. When The Goblin premeditated any operation, no matter how simple or complicated it was, he always had a backup plan. This time our agency was not directly involved with the scheme. Some other people planned the whole thing, however, it looked as though something was not working for them and the situation seemed to be getting out of control. Director Goldberg was urgently called upon by his superiors to help them fix things. But first, let me just give you the whole story in a nutshell.

Our Government Officials spent a lot of time and money trying to secure a few deals in the politically troubled, but rich in energy and natural resources, region which is located on a distant continent in a different part of the world. It was a clear sign that with the potential "go ahead" of this agreement, both countries would significantly benefit economically and financially from the joint venture. The transaction appeared to be "a sure" and "just a matter of time" thing, when suddenly a third party got involved. This unexpected, nasty and unwanted player tried to break the almost done arrangement by bringing up a lot of garbage on the surface and unfairly blaming our country for all their own troubles and everything else. In addition to the trash talks and unjust competition, this challenger offered the locals some "really sweet deal" on their expertise in the area of the development of natural resources. Furthermore, these pitiless people proposed some other supplementary advantages, such as the possibility of buying modern Weaponry at low prices. From an economical point of view this proposal was "like piss against the wind" for that spiteful player. But the economics probably did not matter much to them at the preliminary stage of the initiative, because the natural resources, energy and arms treaty would give these folks the ability to control that country, and with power comes everything else. Also, this possible military hardware deal would certainly break the peace, which we all worked so hard to achieve, as well as the balance and stability in the region, and will put that whole neighboring area at risk and in danger. Any sober and adequate person would agree that we could not let that happen. And, as I mentioned earlier, our side did not want to lose the money that had already been spent on research and negotiations; the financial and economical part of the deal is still important to us.

When all the talks about the joint venture first started, the mediators from our nation were mostly actual business people: economists, accountants, managers of different levels and some other administrative officials. The available resources of many Intelligence agencies were not utilized. Someone in the position to make decisions did not see the need for it at that time. This was a mistake. And this was a lesson. Usually I, as an average person, think good of people too, until proven otherwise. The view of the professional Intelligence Officer is different. There is always a sign "proceed with caution" somewhere in the brain. And now, after the unexpected appearance of the third party, we are the ones who have to fix everything and deliver the projected results. The way to turn the state of affairs to our advantage again was this: at that stage of the negotiation process the head of the country of interest was uncertain and hesitant. The vicious move by the third party played its part. And that leader was the one and only who makes decisions for his country. Of course that man in power has many advisors and consultants, but he is the prime decision maker. And as I understood the situation before our agency's participation was like fifty – fifty: a fifty percent chance that the deal goes to the right business people and a fifty percent chance it would go to the opposition. The numbers look good, if you do not know the whole agenda. The unconvinced foreign leader needed assurance from the leader of our country, as well as from the government that they would not let him down if something does not work or goes wrong. Probably, the experienced man did not want to be left one on one with the powerful and aggressive third party.

I do not think that it was too difficult for our side to give those prospective business partners the necessary guarantees. But what is simple in theory is not always the same uncomplicated matter in reality. In reality, our side could not go through the regular rules of trade relationships that are commonly accepted throughout the modern world and are usually backed up by governments and by the first men or women of democratic countries, even though our administration representatives were involved in the prospective deal from the beginning. I am not sure of the exact reason for such behavior by our side; maybe this type of a transaction is against the domestic or international law or maybe this conduct by our delegates was due to some political reasons (this is exactly what I think personally), but the business deal did not go through yet. And the head of our state supported the trade agreement all the way unofficially, but somehow he cannot go out there and publicly announce that we are in and are ready to guarantee the whole lot to the likely partners. And by the way, you cannot promise or guarantee everything. This is common sense. Even the richest insurance companies do not cover the whole thing, despite the fact that people pay money to them for their services. So, both sides are stuck at a certain point of the negotiation process, trying to find a solution. Actually it was just our side which tried hard to move forward. The other party at that time considered other options which were proposed by our opposition. So, to secure the deal for our country some of the government officials eventually figured out that they need an urgent and qualified source of help and decided to bring new players into the game, some extraordinary professional people who know what to do in situations like this. Director Goldberg, as he usually does, found the solution. Being one of the nation's most experienced men in dealing with similar issues and after getting familiar with the sensitive details of the matter, The Goblin proposed an interesting and simple combination. The director, as his high profile position required, knew the fact that in the upcoming future the leader of our state is expected to address the United Nations General Assembly. In order to demonstrate to the potential partners the complete approval of the deal on the previously agreed terms by our side, The Goblin offered their representatives to come up with some phrase or a sentence, which our leader will include in his speech while addressing the U.N General Assembly. The speech will be broadcasted throughout the entire modern world. When our likely partners will witness that the phrase was pronounced, then they will know that the deal was approved by the first man as well as by the government and we are ready to proceed. Of course both parties understood that this move might look very secretive and unofficial in some way, but it will give the prospective partners the desired assurance that we would not let them down, no matter what. We value our friends and keep our promises. It was not a surprise to me at all that the solution formula offered by director Goldberg was accepted. Sometime later, through our own communication channels, I received new instructions from The Goblin and the key phrase, which I had to pass on to the right person. That right person is the speechwriter for our nation's leader, to be exact. The expression was the following: "Bridges across oceans and cultures..."

I did my part, the slogan was delivered. It took me some

time and diplomatic skills to explain why and when this particular motto has to be included into the document, but otherwise everything went well and smooth. On the specified day, even though I knew that I did my best and no one can blame me for anything, I was still worried. I turned the TV set on a little bit earlier than the program was supposed to start and stuck to it like glue. And yet as it often happens, the big moment came unexpectedly. I listened to every word that was said by our leader and when the key phrase was pronounced, it was a huge relief for me. We won. Now it was the time for our business people to close the deal.

When director Goldberg returned back from his voyage, he thanked me for the work well done. The Goblin said: "Thanks for the great job Serge. I knew I can count on you."

I answered: "Sir, it was you and your brilliant idea all the way. I just served as a bridge across some empty space connecting different organizations and dots. And thank you for the opportunity to contribute. It is nice to be a part of something that big."

A short time later the director informed me that our contribution to the project played its part and the country of interest signed all the necessary business papers. Everyone was happy, except the third party. These people could not prove anything, but still blamed our innocent side for the self-governing decision made by someone else, meaning by our new partners. Well, it was a business deal and in such matters people of commerce, before making their choice, usually consider all the known factors and propositions, including the safety measures, expenses, potential profit, and so on. You cannot blame a customer at the convenience store for choosing the best products available. You help them to choose.

One day at work, when it was the time for me to go on a lunch break, Kristina showed up at my desk and invited me to share a meal with her and to talk. I did not mind, on the opposite I enjoy having conversations with smart and elegant people. The only thing I asked Kristina is to go to a shopping mall with me and have our talk and meal there. I needed to buy some kind of a gift for someone special to me.

At the mall, after Kristina helped me to select a nice piece of jewelry, explaining why this type of an ornament is better and more practical than the other one, we went to the food court. Surprisingly there were many people at the eating place at that time of the day. Anyway, we bought some food and were able to find an empty table somewhere in the distant corner. We just started our meal when suddenly I heard: "Hi Mr. Chicken. Hi Ms. Jones. How are you? Nice to meet you again." It was Ena and her father. Probably noticing a look of surprise on my face Ena quickly corrected herself: "Sorry, Mr. Chic, I did not mean to offend you. It is just easier this way for me to remember names when I connect them to something that is already familiar to me, but I end up saying it automatically. Sorry Sir."

I replied: "Do not worry Ena, everything is good."

The young lady and her father were shopping at the mall and came to the food court to take a break and eat something. We had two more empty chairs at the table and offered these kind and strong people to join our little party. All four of us were chewing carefully. Kristina and Ena had some fruit salads, yogurt and juice. The kid's father and I had meat, wheat and something sweet. Somehow the conversation, even though Kristina and I tried to avoid it, turned to the expected direction. We started talking about Romeo. The depressed father, who by the way looked much better today than when I saw the man last time, said: "First I thought that my son's knife injuries were aimed at us, his parents, to make us support any life decision, be it religious or something else, that Romeo had to make. Now, sometime later and after reviewing the past events in my head, I think different. Today I honestly believe that this "self-harm case" was a form of preparation for parents: someone knew that "the jump" was coming…"

No need to say that Kristina and I were listening to the man with full attention. It was obvious that the kid's father is still in pain. At the same time I had a whole bunch of diverse thoughts in my head. I was thinking: "There are a lot of strange things here. For example: the suicide note was different. People, who commit suicides, usually leave notes explaining their actions. And that was the case with Romeo. But what is dissimilar and needs some further investigation is the fact that most people become victims of something, for example bullying at school or similar and they, those sufferers, cannot tolerate it any longer and suicide for them is the only escape route from their painful environment and reality to, as they believe, somewhere nice and quiet. In Romeo's case he did not blame anyone or anything, on the opposite; it seems like the young man assumed that he was saving a little girl, his sister, by sacrificing his own life. In the last note that Romeo wrote he asked his family to understand him and promised to be at the Heaven's Gate to meet everyone when their time comes. This does not stay in line with the usual pattern of suicides. We probably have to ask for the opinion of other behavior experts on this case to clarify the known details. Kristina shared her point of view already and as I understood from her words, we do not have enough data to make any conclusions."

In the meanwhile the gentleman continued: "Please do not think that I am crazy. Yes, I am still in pain, but my conscience is perfectly clear. It is just every day I have this little thought in my head: what if Ena is right? I still keep in mind our last conversation with you after my son's funeral and I remember everything I told you. Let me just jog your memory. My daughter Ena has a very good eye for details and she noticed that my son's coffin was closed and not one of us saw the dead body. Also, she called for the additional information to the medical professional who was supposed to do an autopsy on my son. The doctor in charge replied that the autopsy was not necessary; the cause of death was too obvious. Well, maybe it was too obvious to him, but to us, Romeo's family members, this doctor's story sounds suspicious. There were some other minor and major discrepancies. Anyway, based on the results of her personal investigation, Ena suggested that there is still a good chance that my son is alive."

Kristina and I looked at each other with understanding. We knew that the pain of losing a child would not go away that quickly and easily. Most likely it will never go away at all. But time has a good way of healing old wounds. And sometimes when a distressed person talks to others and is willing to let go, this helps significantly. Today the kid's father talks nonsense, but tomorrow... Who knows what will happen tomorrow? Despite seeing looks of disbelief on our faces, the gentleman continued: "Maybe Ena is right, maybe my son did not die in that horrific accident and it was some kind of a secret operation, something like a witness protection program or similar, done by one of the many

Intelligence Services of this country? Maybe Romeo, at this very moment, while we are talking, is going through some professional and effective training to become a Super Spy? And also everyone forgot about the neighbor, who was there, at that house, when my son stabbed himself five times with a knife into his chest, very close to his heart. Considering the fact that there was a lot of blood, but the wounds were not deep, almost causing no harm, it raises the question if someone else made those cuts or was standing nearby just in case to make sure that everything is done according to the protocol and some terrifying plan? Sometimes I think that the mysterious neighbor, who could easily be an associate of some secret service or police, working undercover, did those slashes himself to help Romeo to play his part in that unexplainable game."

The man stopped for a moment, looked at all of us, then reached into his pocket and pulled out a piece of paper. "Here," he said, passing the paper to me and continued: "This is a list of my thoughts and possible reasons on the whole situation regarding my son. Please read it. I included in it all the likely and crazy ideas. I am sure you will understand what I am trying to say here. And of course if you would like, you can make a copy of it."

I thanked the gentleman, moved my chair closer to Kristina, so she could see the content of the paper as well, and started reading. Here is what was on the list.

A. The money issue.

After being released from jail, Romeo applied for the disability support program. And by the way his application was approved. When a young and a healthy kid, who has many years of life in front of him, does not want to work and asks for money, then this move could easily make someone in charge of the program's funds upset and angry. It is much cheaper for these people, using the available resources, to make the unwanted person who is on the program believe that God is calling for them and that God asked them to prove their love for Him by jumping from a high-rise building.

B. Investment and conspiracy.

I was not born yesterday and of course I heard that some secret organizations have developed certain tools to find and hire new people. Even though this theory may sound foolish, I still believe that this underground case scenario is very possible. When some powerful and sneaky organization picks up young men and women to secretly use their advanced technology and know-how on these innocent and juvenile people in order to make those kids some kind of zombies, it is called a conspiracy. They do it to control the kids by making them today's or future servants. Of course there is a chance that this could be some other party pulling the strings behind the scene. There are so many undisclosed initiatives by people in power out there, of which average folks are unaware of. The smart government invests in the future of the country in which it rules; they do not just cover holes in a budget. They prevent bad things from happening and that particular program is one of the methods to do just that.

C. A system's failure.

Something we do not know had happened to my son in jail. Romeo was in there many times before and he was okay, if you can say so, then what happened this time? I have a few versions. 1. Nothing suspicious or unusual, a natural course of life, not a plot, there was not any third party involvement, no psychoactive drugs, the kid just became tired, upset, and paranoid and this led to the "jump". 2. There is a real possibility that for whatever reason some people, maybe even Romeo's cellmates, shared drugs with him. The healthy kid simply became a drug addict and the crises, which led to the "jump", had happened. 3. Other. I do not have enough information today to make any conclusions. If you keep your mind open, then you can see that there could be a number of different possibilities to cause harm to a naive young man in such conditions. 4. Immigration could easily become Cultural Shock not just for a particular kid, but for any human. Today we do not know if any psychoactive drugs and/or hypnosis were used, except for the Marijuana case involving a neighbor. The unfortunate combination of Cultural Shock and chemical elements in the brain (Marijuana, food, other meds) created a confused and vulnerable mind – a good opportunity to brainwash a person under such circumstances. This could lead to the "jump" as well.

D. A conspiracy theory (Ena's version).

My son is still alive. He was secretly drafted by some Intelligence Agency or a similar organization. Why these mysterious people would need him to be dead on paper? There are could be a number of reasons and explanations. For example: the nature of the work, the money and insurance issue, unwritten law of undercover operations (to deny everything in the case of failure), my son's new religion, Romeo's background and Martial Arts skills and so on. The kid speaks a couple of foreign languages and these dangerous people could easily train him and then send him back to his native country with a covert mission or they could even throw him into the risky whirlpool of one of the countries of his new religion with some dangerous assignment.

E. Religion.

A few people from one of many religious organizations, as they usually do, tried to recruit the kid to become a future member of that group. Also, it is possible that these pious folks were just sharing their views with Romeo, like they were really trying to help the young man in their own way to find his way towards God. And there is nothing unusual in that situation, except the fact that the kid repeatedly pronounced the phrase: "The end of the World is coming". And we know what happened after that. Also, there is still a good chance that religion was used as a cover to distract any possible investigation involving my son by misleading us into the wrong direction. There are some known incidents when one or other religious society or sect clandestinely used psychotropic substances to influence its members or prospective members and to deprive these associates of their Will for the purpose of having power over them and to control their actions. This might be the case as well.

F. All of the above.

When Kristina and I finished reading the paper, the gentleman, acting shy, volunteered to make a copy for us. I needed a copy of it because I am a professional and this information, even if it may seem extreme and unnecessary today, could lead us to something valuable tomorrow. Kristina probably needed the paper to do one of those evaluations for her research on the topic of psychology. When we were leaving the food court and said good bye to Ena and her father, the gentleman said: "You can pick the correct answer for yourself. I made my choice already."

Serge and Roman Lapytski
December 03, 2012